A Family to Keep

Susan Gable

Copyright Page
This book was previously published under the title
The Family Plan.

Copyright © 2017 by Susan Guadagno
First Printing Infinite Daydreams
ISBN-13: 978-0-9967992-3-2
ISBN-10: 0-9967992-3-0
Cover © The Killion Group, Inc.

Susan Gable

Special thanks to

Kate Marquart, who answered a million questions about leukemia, aplastic anemia and bone marrow transplants. I couldn't have done it without you. Any errors are mine.

Jen, for sharing the details of life with a stitched cervix, flat on your back in bed for months during a pregnancy.

Jen and Diana, as always, thank you for your support, encouragement and friendship. For talking me off the ledge when I needed it, and for slaying the Doubt Demons.

CHAPTER ONE

MEN WERE UNRELIABLE creatures at best. Toxic at worst.

A few—very few—could be delightful and amusing in discrete, small doses. But a woman with an education and career, a well-stocked toolbox and easy-to-follow home repair book, along with a steady supply of batteries for her B.O.B.—battery operated boyfriend—didn't actually *need* one.

Certainly Dr. Amelia Young didn't.

And yet, here she was. In North East, Pennsylvania, a little town outside of Erie. About to finish a quest she'd started a month ago, a search that included private investigators whose methods she suspected involved computer hacking. She didn't know, didn't care to know, only cared about the results: this address.

Another step forward in her larger plan.

She eased her Jeep Liberty into the parking lot on the side of the massive old Victorian. The house perched on a bluff, overlooking Lake Erie. The October dawn streaked the clouds over the vineyard across the street with bright rosy hues. The leaves on the towering oak in the front yard had begun to turn, their tips blazing scarlet. According to her reports, the building had once been a bed-and-breakfast.

Well, Amelia wasn't in need of either.

After pulling into a space alongside a green Dumpster, she

jerked the gearshift into Park. Rehearsing several more possibilities of what to say to the donor, she climbed out.

Sets of sawhorses dotted the front lawn, and another pair graced the wide wraparound porch. Lumber was stacked near the front door. The construction crew she'd observed late yesterday afternoon was nowhere to be seen as yet. Exactly how she'd planned.

The last thing she wanted was an audience for this.

The doorbell chimed as she leaned on the button. "Don't say Jordan's name," she reminded herself softly. "No gender-specific pronouns. No unnecessary information. Get in, get what you came for, and get out."

Several minutes and a few more *ding-dongs* later, muttered curses accompanied the sharp click of the dead bolt on the other side of the large double door. "Damn it, I told you guys not before nine today! It's the freakin' crack of dawn. I catered a party last night and..."

The deep voice trailed off as the door opened.

Leaving Amelia staring at a lean, rippled torso, dusted with dark hair that meandered down to an unbuttoned-but-zipped pair of faded jeans. Meandered down to...

Her face heated. Batteries were *so* not included with *that*. *Good morning to you, too.*

Amelia lifted her gaze—and forced herself not to step backward.

She was looking into her daughter's aquamarine eyes, at her daughter's strong jawline—in a decidedly masculine, sensual face, rough with five o'clock shadow.

The edges of his mouth curved, revealing a deep dimple in his right cheek. He'd caught her staring and found it amusing.

"You're not the construction guys."

She shook her head. "No. I'm not."

"You're way better looking, that's for sure. Much easier on the eyes this early. Can I help you?"

"Y-yes," she stammered, then cleared her throat and straightened her shoulders. "At least, I hope so. You're Finnegan Hawkins, right?"

"Finn. Last time I checked, yeah." The confident, borderline-smug smile faded, replaced with a wary expression. "Why?"

"The Finn Hawkins who, thirteen years ago, was a sperm donor for American Fertility Labs in New York City?"

For a long moment, he stared at her. Her stomach tightened, certain he was about to deny it. But there was no denying that jaw, or those eyes.

Finn Hawkins was her daughter's father.

"Freakin' hell." He dragged his hand over his face. "I'm going to need coffee for this conversation, aren't I?"

"Probably."

He muttered a few more choice curses. "It hasn't been eighteen years."

"No, it hasn't."

"I'm supposed to be anonymous. I opted to stay anonymous even after eighteen years."

"Sorry about that."

"You don't look very sorry."

Perceptive guy. Because she wasn't. Not in the least. She'd do what needed to be done, no matter what it took, no matter who else got trampled in the process. Though she could understand his desire to remain unknown—she'd certainly never wanted to meet him—it didn't matter. Jordan was counting on her. "Really, Mr. Hawkins, I—"

He held up a hand. "Coffee first. Guess you'd better come in." He opened the door wider, then turned. From his left shoulder and muscular back, the tattoo of a white tiger with blue eyes and bared fangs glared at her.

Well. That was a surprise. Totally not what she'd expected from the sperm donor she'd chosen based on his profile, which had indicated that at twenty-two, he'd already obtained a bachelor's degree in business, with a 3.89 GPA, and was pursuing further education. An IQ solidly above-average. Serious, well-thought-out responses on the essay questions.

The rest of him fit. Thirteen years later, now thirty-five, Finn Hawkins was still tall and lean, no spare tire or love handles in sight. Honestly, if you were going to choose a man to stud for you, this prime specimen—Mr. Sex Walking— would do nicely. Had done nicely.

Pity there hadn't actually been any sex.

The blue eyes and short-cropped walnut hair matched her own coloring, exactly as she'd wanted in a donor. And it was thick. At least Jordan wouldn't have to worry about passing on premature hair loss to any future grandchildren.

Amelia swallowed hard. Not prone to superstition, she still mentally crossed her fingers that Jordan would have a chance to have kids of her own one day.

And may she never have to face what I'm going through right now.

"Are you coming, or what?" he called over his shoulder. "If not, shut the door so I can go back to bed."

"I'm right behind you." She pulled the door closed and

scurried to catch up with him as he strode down the main hallway of the house.

She barely had time to register the dark wooden staircase, or the rooms off either side of the foyer, each littered with tools and building materials.

They passed several other doorways before reaching the back, where the hall opened into an enormous kitchen that ran the width of the house. Amelia stopped in the archway. "Wow. Nice."

He grunted what she assumed was thanks.

In this stunning combination of home and commercial kitchen, the scent of *new* still hung in the air. There were glossy tile floors and marble countertops. A large island work space, a raised serving counter, and two stools at one end. An eight-burner stove with a double oven beneath it, and another double oven mounted in the wall beside it. The stainless steel appliances gleamed, including the commercial dishwashing station in the far corner.

The tiger stretched as Finn reached into a cabinet, pulling out what she assumed was his precious coffee. Just as well. She wanted him fully awake. Bad enough she had to go to a complete stranger for help. No way she wanted to repeat herself. Especially since she still hadn't figured out what to say.

A grinding whir was followed by the sharp scent of coffee, which he dumped unceremoniously into a filter basket before jamming it into the coffeemaker.

She slipped onto one of the tall stools at the island. Without another word to her, he pulled out two mugs, plunking one down in front of her.

"Oh, really, that's not—"

"Indulge me. I don't like to drink alone. If you'd prefer tea..."

"Coffee is fine, thanks."

"Good." He opened the oversize, side-by-side refrigerator. "You like cheesecake?"

"Cheesecake?"

"Breakfast of champions. Gotta have something to go with the coffee. Plain or strawberry sauce?"

"Plain."

Finn Hawkins slipped the plate in front of the woman and turned away quickly, before she could see that his hands shook like a drunk who'd been dry for less than twenty-four hours. He returned to stare at the dark brew streaming into the pot, not certain how he was going to serve without spilling. He sure as hell didn't need a jolt of caffeine to wake up. Ever since she'd said "sperm donor" and "American Fertility Labs" he'd been wide-awake.

"I don't intend to disrupt your life, Mr. Hawkins—"

"And yet here you are." He carried the coffee to the island, managed to pour it without incident.

The woman sat a little straighter. "Thank you." She spooned raw sugar from the bowl. "Yes, here I am."

"I take it that you're, uh, we, that is..." Oh, great, he sounded like an utter ass.

"I have a child who was created with your donation."

Finn tried to hide the fact that all the air had vanished from his lungs. A child. She'd given birth to his child. Which was what he'd suspected.

But he still didn't even know this pull-the-rug-out-from-under-him woman's name.

Recovering his breath, he guessed that was as good a place as any to start. "You seem to have the advantage here. I'm Finn, and you are?"

"Amelia."

"Just Amelia?"

She nodded. "I think that would be best. Like I said, I'm not really interested in disrupting your life. You wanted to stay anonymous, and I can understand that. But unfortunately, I had to find you."

He dragged the empty stool from beside her, positioning himself on the opposite side of the island. "Okay, Amelia. I figure you must want something. So here's the million-dollar question. What?"

She paused, then set down her mug, rummaging in her purse. "Nothing more than you gave thirteen years ago." Plastic crinkled and she placed a wrapped specimen cup next to her coffee.

"What the hell?" Finn jumped up. "Whoa, whoa. Wait a minute here. Number one, I gave at the office. Number two, I don't do that kind of thing anymore."

"Mr. Hawkins, as I said, this is urgent. I wouldn't be here otherwise."

"Lady, the sperm bank has plenty of other little swimmers for you to choose from. Go through the catalog and pick someone else."

"It has to be you."

"Why?" He slowly sank back to his seat, eyeing the specimen cup warily. Did she seriously expect him to simply pick the thing up, excuse himself to the bathroom, and return with it filled? Good grief, the woman was a nutcase. No wonder she'd had to resort to a sperm bank to have a child.

"I need a full biological sibling for my child. A half-sib won't do."

A horrifying suspicion struck him. But she was asking for sperm. Not blood. Not a kidney. Not, God forbid, bone marrow. "Why?"

She twirled a strand of shoulder-length hair around her index finger. "This doesn't have to be a big deal," she said softly. "Just give me what I came for, and you never have to hear from me again."

"I wasn't supposed to be hearing from you *now*. And yes, it *is* a big deal. You're asking me to father another child for you."

"No, I'm not." She nudged the container in his direction. "I'm asking you to fill it and forget this ever happened. Just like you did thirteen years ago."

"It's not like you're asking to borrow a cup of sugar."

"It doesn't have to be any more complicated than that."

Finn sighed. "Look, I'm flattered you're so thrilled with my genes that you want more of them. But I shouldn't have done it then, and I'm not going to do it again now."

The color drained from her face and she propped her arms on the counter, staring into her coffee. "Oh. That's...that's unexpected."

"What? That I don't believe in indiscriminate reproduction anymore?"

She looked up. "You believed in it thirteen years ago."

"Thirteen years ago, I was young and stupid. I hadn't thought it through. It was an impulsive, crazy thing to do." Of course, crazy and impulsive defined most of his life. He'd applied and been accepted to grad school, but, inspired by Greg's success as a comic-book artist, and their parents' grudging acceptance of his brother's somewhat unorthodox pursuits, Finn had chosen culinary school. His life had been one kitchen after another, one location after another, one relationship after another....

Until he ended up here, back home.

"Look, Mr. Hawkins—"

"Finn. I think, given the situation, you can use my first name."

"All right. Finn. Is there a woman whose permission you need for this?"

There was one woman in his life who *would* care.

He snorted. "Yeah, my mom. And she would rip me a new one if she found out I'd created grandbabies she never knew about." Which was why he'd only donated twice before his conscience had slammed the door—and his zipper—shut.

Amelia's eyebrows drew together. "This is *not* your mother's grandbabies we're talking about. We are talking about *my* child. You and your mom have nothing to do with it."

"I'm pretty sure I have something to do with it, or you wouldn't be here." He shook his head. "I'm sorry. I can't. I won't."

The muscle on the side of her jaw twitched. She dug in her purse again, slapped a checkbook on the counter. "I'll pay you. The clinic paid, right?"

"You're joking?"

"Do I look like I'm joking?"

No. She didn't. And he wasn't sure how to take that. "Money isn't the point. It wasn't the point then." He sighed.

"I'm sorry."

She slid from the stool and stalked the length of the kitchen, stopping at the back door. She leaned her head against the edge of the frame. Her shoulders slumped.

Ah, hell. He left his own chair, went to stand behind her. "You're not crying, are you?" he murmured. "'Cause there's no crying in the kitchen."

"No," she snapped. "I'm not crying."

"Why is this so important to you? What's the big need for a full biological sibling?"

Her blue eyes, a shade darker than his own, were red-rimmed, but no tears fell as she turned abruptly to face him.

"My child's life is at stake. And I will do whatever it takes to save h—uh, my child. *Whatever* it takes."

Finn's chest tightened. "Why? What's wrong?"

"Severe aplastic anemia," she said.

"What's that?"

"It's a blood disorder. Her body doesn't make enough new blood cells."

"That's serious?"

"It's often fatal. Treatment can help control it for a while, but the only chance my child has for a cure is a bone marrow transplant—"

The room tilted around him with those three words.

"—and there's no match in the database. We need a matching sibling."

"Shitdamnhell." He raked his hand through his hair. "I'm sorry."

She pressed her lips tightly together, gave a quick jerk of her head. Her eyes filled again.

He'd always been a sucker for a strong woman's tears. The determined way she struggled for control tied his guts into knots.

He pulled her against his chest.

She stiffened for a moment, then leaned into him. Finn wrapped his arms around her, stroking her silky hair. Vanilla. She smelled of vanilla.

Something deep inside him warmed. A primitive need to protect, to help this woman who, despite her protests to the contrary, had given birth to *his* child. "I'm so, so sorry."

She rested her head against his shoulder.

He held her for a few moments. When she eased back, he let her go.

He crossed the kitchen to rummage in the cabinet beneath the island. Pulling out the bottle of Bailey's, he dumped a liberal dose into his mug. He turned it toward hers as she joined him. "You probably need this more than I do."

She waved him off. "Need it, yes. But..." Her mouth twitched. "I'm hoping to get pregnant soon, so none for me. Coffee is already pushing it." She picked up her mug, took a long drink.

"How do you get this anemia thing?"

"The doctors aren't sure."

"Is it genetic?"

"Sometimes."

He put the bottle away, the tremors returning to his hands with a vengeance. His worst nightmare had come true. His child was out there, sick, with a disease his DNA may have transmitted. Of course, he hadn't known at the time. His brother Ian's bout with leukemia had occurred shortly after

Finn had donated his sperm. After the diagnosis, he'd begun to worry. What if?

Now, *what if* was standing in his kitchen. She wasn't a nutcase, after all. Just a desperate mother trying to save her child's life.

He knew a thing or three about determined mothers, having watched his own with Ian. Every single sibling, eleven of them in all, had been tested. Derek and Kyle had matched. Kyle's age, only thirteen at the time, had led to Derek being designated the donor for Ian.

Except Ian hadn't survived long enough for the transplant. Double pneumonia, in conjunction with his weakened immune system, had cut his fight short.

Which meant Finn—and the rest of the clan—didn't match Amelia's child, either, since they were all listed in the Bone Marrow registry as a result of the tests.

"What if the new baby doesn't match?"

"They prescreen the embryos before they implant them. They'll match."

"Oh." He settled back onto the stool and waited for her to do the same, then leaned across the island to clasp her hand. Her fingers were cold and clammy despite having been wrapped around the cup of hot java. He gave them a quick squeeze. "Okay. Tell me the whole story."

"There's nothing more to tell. I need you to help save my child. Will you?"

Anger surged through him. "What kind of a man do you take me for?"

She freed her hand from his grasp. "Mr. Hawkins—"

He glared at her.

"Finn. I have no clue what type of man you are. Hopefully, you're not the kind who can turn his back on someone who needs you." She glanced down.

"You're not used to asking for help." He could see it in the proud way she held her head, her shoulders.

"No. But I'll beg if I have to."

"You don't have to."

Her head jerked up. "Really? You'll do it?"

She wasn't asking him to be a father. Amelia's emphatic references to "her child" drove that fact home. Not that he wanted to be a dad at this point in his life.

He had enough to handle right now, getting the restaurant ready to open without adding a family-size side dish of complications.

But if the only way to save one child was to create another... Did he have a choice?

"Yeah, I'll do it."

###

Ten minutes later, Finn found himself upstairs, in the bathroom attached to his bedroom, warily eyeing the specimen cup he'd unwrapped and set on the counter. He paced the small space—one and a half steps one way, one and a half back. Sinking to perch on the edge of the bathtub, he scrubbed his palm over his face.

Think dirty thoughts. Imagine naked women.

But the only image that came to mind was the troubled blue eyes of the woman who waited in his kitchen, and the only thoughts were of his unknown, unnamed, sick child. He didn't even know the gender!

He stared down at his zipped fly. "Hell, at least the clinic provided magazines."

He could always raid Hayden's room. No doubt his younger brother, who'd moved to the new place with him following Greg's engagement, had an old *Playboy* or two stashed somewhere. Hayden insisted *Playboy* was classier than surfing the Internet.

Thank God Hayden, known within the family, not always affectionately, as Jabber Jaw, had already left for work.

That train of thought wasn't helping Finn, either.

What he needed was inspiration. Motivation.

He smiled wryly.

His best inspiration always had been found in the kitchen.

CHAPTER TWO

"HOW'S THE WEATHER in Boston, Mom?"

Cell phone pressed to her ear, Amelia stared out the kitchen's back window, through the enclosed porch at the stunning view of Lake Erie. "Nice. Sunny. A bit warmer than home." Home was Caribou, Maine, located as far north as you could get on the eastern coast of the States. She'd left New York City when Jordan was an infant for a more wholesome, healthy environment in which to raise her child. *So much for healthy.*

"Uh-huh. And how's the chiropractic conference?"

"Same as usual. Kind of boring, but necessary."

Her daughter snorted. "Mom, you suck at lying."

Amelia's chest tightened. "What? Why would you say that? Accusing your own mother of—"

"Google. According to the Internet, it's raining in Boston this morning. And there's no chiropractic conference there right now. Where *are* you?"

"I—I'm taking that computer away from you!" She'd bought Jordan the laptop, complete with all the bells and whistles including built-in Wi-Fi, for her thirteenth birthday. Supposedly to let her do things while they waited in medical offices, or on occasion, in the hospital. She hadn't figured her daughter would use it to spy on her. *Kids.*

"Mom, you never lie to me, not even about the scary medical stuff. What's going on?"

Amelia fumbled for something to tell her.

"Ohmigod. You found him, didn't you? You found my father."

Amelia clenched her teeth before answering, repeating something she'd told Jordan umpteen hundred times. "He is *not* your *father*. He's the sperm donor responsible for half your DNA."

"Whatever, Mom. Not the point. What's he look like? Do I look like him? Is he on board with the plan? *Where are you?*"

Door hinges squeaked. Amelia turned to see the man in question coming out the back staircase he'd climbed twenty minutes earlier. Only now he wore a form-hugging white T-shirt and clutched *the cup*.

She needed to get that, Jordan's lifeline, to the Erie Bay-front Fertility Clinic, which had agreed—at a price, of course—to process it for her and ship it to the clinic she was using in Portland, Maine.

"Mom?"

"Gotta run, babe. I'll call you later."

"Mom! Mom! Take a picture and send it to me!"

Amelia ended the call and flicked the ringer off, crossing to meet Finn by the island. She shoved her cell into her purse and reached for the container. "Now that's what I call service. Thanks."

"Don't thank me yet."

"What?"

He shook his head, then inclined it in the direction of her hand.

The cup was still empty. "You changed your mind?"

"No." Faint pink flushed his cheeks, highlighting his rough

morning stubble. He narrowed his eyes, appraising her. His attention slid from her face to linger slightly lower. Beneath the cream turtleneck, her breasts tightened in response.

The corner of his mouth twitched, and his gaze dropped still lower. The visual caress glided over her waist and hips.... She tried to speak, but had to unglue her tongue from the roof of her suddenly dry mouth first. "Why are you looking at me like that?"

His attention snapped back to her face. That slow grin appeared, along with his dimple. "I want to kiss you."

The temperature in the room shot up, as if all his ovens were running full blast with the doors open. She took a step back. "I..."

He advanced on her. "I've given you a child. You've asked for another one. I don't think a kiss is too much to ask in return, do you?"

"A kiss?"

"I need..."

"Need?" she prompted when he fell silent.

His gaze flickered to the object still clutched in her hand. He cleared his throat. "Yeah. *Need.* A little inspiration... I can't... Aw, hell. Forget it."

The color in his face deepened as he glanced at the floor, all smugness gone. "Oh. *Oh.*" *Adorable.* He needed her help. Being in his arms earlier had been awkward, but the idea of kissing him appealed to her. She didn't plan to stick around to see if he was a toad or a prince. It didn't matter. Just a kiss... "I agree."

His head snapped up. "With what?"

"A kiss isn't too much to ask in return."

"Um..." His Adam's apple jerked as he swallowed hard. "Okay, good." He took another deliberate step in her direction, cat-and-mouse style.

Her stomach somersaulted as she inched away. His eyes smoldered and the sexy, smug smile returned.

Apparently she was a sucker for Finn Hawkins's smile.

By the time her back bumped into the tight corner by the sink, her knees were wobbling and her skin tingled. She set the container down. He planted his hands on the countertop, one on each side of her, stopping short of making body-to-body contact. He dipped his head forward, burying his nose in her hair and inhaling deeply. "Mmm. You smell delicious, Amelia."

She shivered.

He ran the tip of his tongue along the curve of her ear. "Last chance to change your mind," he murmured.

Hell would have to freeze over before she'd deny herself his kiss. "Last chance to change *your* mind," she countered.

A soft chuckle shook his lean, muscled frame as he eased against her.

Every nerve fired to attention. She lifted her chin and closed her eyes.

He brushed his lips over hers, a tentative touch, then hovered. "Arabica coffee." He connected again, this time nibbling on her lower lip.

She surged forward, initiating something far less hesitant, her tongue seeking entrance.

Which he denied. He trailed his mouth along her jawline, then nipped her earlobe. "Not so fast," he murmured. "A kiss...a *woman*...is like a fine meal. Meant to be savored."

"Mmm. Sometimes devouring a fine meal is better."

He laughed, pulling back. "I think I could like you, Amelia No-Last-Name."

She opened her eyes and grinned. "I think I could like you, too, Finn Hawkins. Now, about that kiss..." She clenched his T-shirt in both hands.

He pressed against her, reaching up to grip the back of her neck, and proceeded to kiss her. Thoroughly. *Very, very thoroughly.* Mint masked the lingering flavor of coffee. His mouth...his body...was warm, inviting. It had been way too long since she'd indulged herself, known the bliss of melting into a man.

Sometimes men had their uses.

Like now. She'd never see him again, so why not enjoy this "conception" at least a little?

Her pulse kicked up, and she slid her fingers down his chest, then gripped his belt loops, yanking him even closer. She arched her back, pressing her breasts against his cotton shirt.

"Take your shirt off," she whispered. "I want to touch you."

He groaned against her lips, grinding his arousal into her hip. He drew back to look at her. "You sure about that? If you can't take the heat, Amelia, now would be the time to get the hell out of my kitchen and let me deal with this. "

"I can take the heat. Can you?" She popped the button on his jeans.

His eyes widened.

With a slow grin that mirrored the ones he'd been shooting her since she'd appeared on his front porch, she drew down his zipper, millimeter by millimeter.

"Amelia—"

"You're still wearing your shirt." What he wasn't wearing was anything under his jeans. She took him in her hand. Batteries not needed, for sure. Oh, yes. *This* was what she'd been missing. A warm, responsive, *human* connection.

He bucked, cursing a blue streak and yanking the T-shirt over his head. She let the fingers of her other hand wander the hard planes of his chest and ridged six-pack, the softness of his dark hair contrasting with the firm muscles beneath.

Rational thought fled as he reached under her turtleneck, skimming his palm up her stomach to caress her breast through her satin bra.

An unknown number of breath-stealing moments later, her shirt ended up bunched around her neck, her bra was unfastened, and Finn's mouth—his warm, eager mouth—made the room spin as he feasted on her breasts. One of his hands slipped inside her low-rise jeans, inside her panties...and then inside her.

Damn. She moaned softly.

Finn struggled for control as Amelia stroked him. The woman's response had shocked the hell out of him. He'd worried that asking for a kiss was too pushy. This...this had rocketed way past his meager hope, right into fantasy territory. With his thumb he caressed her, making her tremble and gasp.

"Amelia," he groaned as her hand quickened its exquisite tempo. "I'm close."

"Me, too," she panted. "Please, Finn..."

Oh, hell, he'd warned her. No stopping now. He stroked

her faster, harder, wholly focused on pushing her over the edge. When she gasped his name and pulsed in pleasure against his fingers, fire streaked up his spine, through his stomach...and he surrendered to pleasure.

She purred with contentment.

The afterglow lasted less than a minute.

"Oh my God!" Amelia cried. "Oh my God!"

Finn forced his eyes open, disentangling himself from her garments. "Yeah. I agree. Wow."

"What have we done?" She stared down at her hand.

Rational thought slowly filtered into his rapidly thawing brain. "Uh-oh," he muttered.

"Uh-oh?" She bit down on her lower lip before continuing. "That's all you have to say?"

His gut tightened. "I, uh, gave you a heads-up. You were directing traffic, not me. My hands were full with...other things."

Her jaw set. "You're right. You did. I can't believe I let myself get that carried away."

"I can fix this." He offered her a shaky grin as he zipped up. "Give me a half hour."

She reached under her shirt, around her back, fumbling with her bra clasp.

Finn debated helping her, but she looked like she might strangle him if he touched her again. "I think I have all the inspiration I need."

She thrust the container at him again, then grabbed her purse and sweater. "I'll wait in my car."

Regret coursed through him. "Avoiding temptation?"

She folded her arms over her chest. "I'm sorry I let myself

get carried away."

"I'm not." Their brief encounter had been the most mind-blowing not-actual-sex of his life.

"Typical man."

"What?"

"I said, 'typical man.' At least you didn't ask if it was good for me."

His pride wounded, Finn stepped deliberately close, lowered his head and his voice as he said, "I don't have to ask, darlin'. I know it was."

She blew out a long breath, then shook her head. "God save me from arrogant men. Fill the cup, hotshot. I'll be in the car."

###

Waiting in the vehicle, Amelia found her hands were still shaking a full ten minutes later. Not only had she gotten physically involved with her sperm donor, she'd managed to blow the opportunity to get what she—what Jordan—needed.

Inexcusable.

What if the quality of his second sample wasn't as good as the first? She thought she'd read something along those lines from some brochure in a fertility clinic waiting room—or maybe in some women's magazine.

Amelia took a deep breath and settled back into the car seat.

She'd certainly gotten more than she'd bargained for. The physical attraction...she'd never experienced anything like that before. Plus he'd been tender.

But then again, they all started out that way. First impressions were often deceiving.

Pulling out her cell phone, she found five text messages. All from Jordan. All saying the same thing: Get a picture. I wanna see him.

Amelia had seen more than enough. She fired off a one-word response sure to anger her daughter: No.

She wanted to deliver the sperm to the clinic in Erie, get home and never look back. Her daughter's DNA donor was attractive and sweet and definitely good with his hands.

She would tell Jordan all but the last.

Hopefully, that would be enough. It had to be.

Amelia reclined the seat back in the car, the warm sunshine combined with the still-lingering lethargy of a really good orgasm making her sleepy. She closed her eyes....and awoke to rapping on the window. She bolted upright, hand on the seat lever, making it snap forward to whack her between the shoulder blades.

The construction crew had arrived during her nap, and men milled around the parking lot, toting tools and wood. Finn held aloft a brown paper bag.

Amelia started the car and lowered the window.

"Special delivery to go."

"Thanks." She took the bag, tucking it between her thighs.

He arched a brow. "Interesting place for it."

"It has to be kept warm. Body temp if possible. I hate to..."

"Come and go?" he offered.

She forced her lips together hard, not wanting to smile. "Exactly. Time is ticking and I have to get this to Erie Bayfront Fertility Clinic ASAP." Within an hour was optimal. She'd checked Mapquest and could be there in twenty minutes.

"I didn't even know Erie had a fertility clinic." He leaned on the window ledge. "Amelia, if you need anything..."

"Thank you. But I have what I need now. You can pretend this never happened."

Finn might want to, but how exactly was he supposed to do that? "Will you keep me in the loop about how things go? Send me a note?"

She shook her head.

"An e-mail? A text?"

More negatives. He crouched lower. "Is it a boy or a girl, Amelia? Can't I at least know that? Have a name?"

"No, Finn. I think this way is best. Now I *really* have to run." She laid her hand over his forearm. "Thank you. My child means everything to me. I'd do anything..."

"I can see that."

He straightened and stepped away from the car. She closed the window and backed from the space. She pulled onto the road and disappeared in the distance.

Disappeared as quickly as she'd arrived.

Two hours and change total.

Now he would always wonder about the child he knew was out there. Would he or she survive? Would the new baby be a boy or girl? How would Amelia cope if the bone marrow transplant didn't work? Or if something happened, like it had with Ian, before they could even get that far?

And had the crazy attraction in his kitchen been strictly one-sided?

CHAPTER THREE

Eight Months Later

JORDAN YOUNG FOLLOWED the other passengers through the little airport. It wasn't like she'd get lost. The place only had one baggage belt.

Which she didn't need. All her stuff was in the wheeled backpack—her mother insisted on wheels, made a huge stink about how bad carrying backpacks was on the spine—that Jordan dragged behind her. It wasn't going to be a long trip.

Forget the aplastic anemia. Her *mom* was gonna kill her.

But at least she would meet her father first.

A tall blonde woman holding a sign with Jordan's name on it stood near the revolving door.

The whole plan had been ridiculously easy once she'd finally found the investigator's report about Finn Hawkins— *Finn Hawkins.* He had such a cool name. Plan the escape during the *real* chiropractic conference in Boston. Convince her mother to take her along. Use Mom's TravelEasy online account and stored credit card info to book the flight from Boston to Erie. Use Uber to get her from the airport to her father's restaurant, Fresh.

Ridiculously easy, thanks to the Internet.

Which she'd probably never have access to again.

"Hi. I'm Jordan Young," she said to the sign holder.

The lady did a double take. "Aren't you a little young to be traveling by yourself?"

Jordan shrugged. "I'm thirteen. My parents aren't together. School's out, and it's Dad's turn to have me." Not a lie at all. She and Shelby, her BFF, whose parents actually were divorced and who shuttled her back and forth across the country several times a year, had come up with the cover story.

"Ah," said the driver, nodding. She reached for Jordan's pack. "You want me to take that?"

"No, I've got it."

Outside, Jordan climbed into the backseat of the silver car. "You have the address, right?"

The driver pointed to her phone. "Yep. Fresh. I've been there. I had dinner there a few weeks ago for my birthday."

"How was it?" Jordan asked as they pulled from the curb.

"Great. The food was amazing. I had lamb chops that were probably the best I've ever had."

Jordan smiled. "My father's the chef there."

The driver looked at her in the rear-view mirror. "My compliments to the chef, then."

"I'll tell him. How long will it take to get there?"

"You haven't been here before?"

"No. It's his new place. I haven't been down since he opened it." No lies there, either.

"About twenty minutes. Maybe a half hour."

Exhausted, but too anxious to grab a quick nap, Jordan pulled her cell phone from her bag and shot a text to Shelby: In Erie. What if he hates me?

A few minutes later, Shelby responded: What? Y u think that?

Jordan's fingers flew over the keyboard. IDK. Nerves?

Shelby's answer came faster this time. Worry more bout ur mom. She's gonna b crazy mad!

No kidding. Call u later!

Kk. Send pics. Dying 2 c him!

They'd actually found pictures of him on the Internet. Loads of articles and reviews about him and his cooking had shown up on Google searches. Shelby had a huge crush on him, which sort of creeped Jordan out. Okay, so he was cute. So what? The guy was her *father,* not some movie star. Not even a TV chef.

Jordan stashed her phone and settled back against the seat. They'd gotten onto a highway, leaving her with little to look at. One highway looked much the same as another, from Maine to Boston to Erie, apparently. Road surrounded by trees, broken up by exits, dotted with buildings.

The longer they drove, though, the more her stomach churned.

By the time they pulled into an overflowing parking lot, she was certain her father's first impression was going to be of her racing to the bathroom. Or worse, puking on his shoes.

The driver opened the door for her, and Jordan slid out, handing her a five-dollar bill. Shelby, her personal travel expert, had instructed her on tipping.

"Thanks," the woman said. "Hey, are you all right? You look a bit pale."

Unless she'd had a recent transfusion, pale was normal for her. "Traveling does that to me. Airport food is the pits."

"I'm sure your father can take care of that. Enjoy your visit."

As the car backed onto the road—the packed parking lot made anything else impossible—Jordan shouldered her backpack by one strap and trudged down the sidewalk. At the bottom of the steps, she paused.

Now that she was here, she wasn't so sure about this. He'd been good enough to go along with Mom's "save Jordan" plan, and now Mom was six months pregnant with her brother or sister.

Mom had said he was a nice, kind man. And that, yes, there were certain resemblances between them.

But that had been all she'd said. And her expression always got sort of weird when Jordan asked about him. More than it had before Mom had met him.

Jordan climbed the steps. The door opened into an entryway lined with empty coatracks, and another set of double doors. Inside, tantalizing aromas made her stomach growl. Maybe she was just hungry.

A young woman with shoulder-length dark hair came out of the dining room on the right, several menus clutched to her chest. She wore black pants and a crisp white blouse. "Hi, there," she said to Jordan as she placed the menus on a small wooden podium at the bottom of a wide staircase. "Can I help you? Is the rest of your group still outside?"

Jordan shook her head. "I'm here to see Finn Hawkins, please."

"Chef's really busy right now. Saturdays are kind of crazy." The woman gestured at the room on the opposite side of the foyer, where people clustered around the bar, or small tables, drinks in hand. "All those folks are waiting to be seated. Do you want me to take a message for him?"

Jordan set the backpack on the floor. "Yes. Please tell him his daughter is here to see him."

The hostess's mouth dropped open, then closed with a click. She cocked her head, looking at Jordan from all angles, her blue eyes growing wider and wider. Then she pointed to the stairs. "Why don't you sit there for a minute?"

She whipped a cell phone out of her pocket, turning toward the wall and saying in a low voice, "Hayden? Get down here right now. The front desk, that's where. Yes, now. I don't care if you have a date tonight. I think you're going to want to cancel it." She whirled around again as she set the phone on the podium. "What's your name, sweetie?"

"Jordan."

"Jordan, I'm Kara." The woman took her by the arm, guided her to the stairs. "You look tired. Sit down."

At the top of the staircase, a door opened and closed. Feet hammered down the wooden treads. A muscular man in jeans and a tight red shirt eased past her. "Excuse me. Kara, what's the big emergency? Finn will pitch a fit if he catches me out front on a Saturday night dressed like this."

"How old are you, Jordan?" Kara asked.

"Thirteen."

She grabbed the man who'd come down the stairs by the arm and dragged him toward the hallway—to move out of hearing, Jordan figured. But she had ears like a bat.

"Fourteen years or so ago, did you sleep with someone and tell her you were Finn?"

"What? Did you get into the wine cellar? Fourteen years ago I was eighteen, pipsqueak. You were just a runt."

"I might have been a runt at the time, but I remember you

had an ID in Finn's name so you could get into the 'wine cellars' yourself. You and Ian both. So answer my question."

"No, I did not sleep with anyone and tell her I was Finn. Why the hell would you ask me that?"

"Because it appears someone did. Oh, my God. You don't think it was Ian, do you? After all, he knocked up Ronni about that time. Nick's thirteen, too."

"And Ian took responsibility for his son. Besides, he was crazy about Ronni. He wasn't sleeping around on her."

Although she wasn't quite sure how it all fit in with her father, Jordan filed away the juicy tidbits to share with Shelby later. Kara led the man back over to her. "Hayden, this is Jordan. Finn's daughter."

After an initial double take, Hayden gave her the same long examination Kara had.

Jordan stood up. "Can I please see him now? I've come a long way. And my mother is going to find out I'm here any minute. Not that she can do anything about it right away, but still, I'd like to meet my father before that happens. Please?"

Hayden grinned. "Far be it from me to stand in the way of that. Come on, sweetheart, I'll take you to the kitchen. Let me carry your bag." In a flash, he had her pack over one brawny shoulder and was ushering her down the hall.

"You can't take her to the kitchen now! You'll throw everything into a complete mess." Kara scampered after them. "No offense, Jordan, but really, can't you wait until he's done cooking for the night? Or did you plan to take over, Hayden? God help the customers."

With every step closer, Jordan's feet grew heavier. The hall seemed to expand in front of her, looming longer and longer. Outside the door labeled Women, she stopped.

Hayden bumped her, recoiling with an apology.

She didn't move.

The man stooped down. "You scared?"

She jerked her head once. *Terrified.* She'd imagined this moment her whole life and now that it was here...

"Listen, my brother's a good guy. It'll be okay. If there's one thing that a Hawkins values, it's family. Remember, his bark in the kitchen is way worse than his bite." Hayden gripped her hand and gave it a friendly squeeze.

His brother? That made this man...her uncle. And Kara, who'd called Hayden big brother, her aunt. Jordan's family was growing by leaps and bounds, and she hadn't even met her father yet. "Ready?"

The hallway had stopped getting longer. She nodded.

Finn swirled wasabi sauce along the edge of the seared ahi plate, then slipped it onto the ledge beside the three other entrées. Gina came through the swinging door. "Table four's ready," he told her.

"Thanks." She started stacking the dishes up her arm.

Tracey stood behind the island at the pass, staring at him. "What?" He wiped his hands on the towel tucked into his apron.

"I need the soup and salad for table seven."

"Yeah? So get it. Where the hell is my sous-chef?" Finn bellowed. "Jon!" he hollered at the busboy unloading dishes from a gray tub into the dishwasher tray. "Run outside and tell Marco to put out the butt and get his ass back in here or he's fired!"

"Yes, Chef." The teen darted out the back door.

Finn checked the tickets stuck to the ledge, then hauled open the oversize fridge, gathering two chilled bowls and quickly assembling Caesar salads. Moving them to the pass, he ladled out two bowls of the soup du jour, wiping the rims before setting them up. "Go! And next time, do it yourself if no one else can."

Marco ambled in the back door, followed by the busboy. "Sorry, Finn. What's next?"

"Table nine. One salmon, one ahi. Get the garnish going."

"You got it, boss."

Finn was turning toward the stove when Hayden, in jeans and a T-shirt, came through the swinging door. "Hayden, what the hell were you doing in the front of my house dressed like that?" he demanded.

"See, told you," Hayden said. Finn had already grabbed his fish from the fridge and was firing the entrées. He dashed some oil into a pan.

"Finn?" Kara said.

"What's up? Everything okay out there? Everybody happy?" He didn't turn to look. His baby sister, who also worked as an elementary teacher, ran the front of the house at night like she ran her fourth-grade classroom. No nonsense.

"Finn, there's someone here who'd like to meet you."

He glanced over his shoulder to see Hayden and Kara, at the far end of the work island, sensibly out of the traffic flow. They flanked a petite girl who looked too old to be one of Kara's students, but not old enough to be applying for a job. "What's kitchen rule number two?"

"No customers in the kitchen."

"Exactly. I'm happy to come to the dining room. Let me get these entrées out and—"

"I'm not a customer." The girl's voice, thin and reedy like she was, shook. "Wow, it's hot in…" Her eyes rolled back.

"Catch her, catch her! She's fainting!" Finn yelled at Hayden. His brother grabbed for the kid. "That's why customers aren't allowed in the kitchen!"

"She's not a customer," Hayden repeated, easing the girl to the floor. "She's your daughter."

"My *what?*" The kitchen fell into relative silence, the sizzle of the fish in the pan now audible.

"I said she's your daughter. At least, that's what she told us. You gotta admit she's got the Hawkins jaw."

"And your eyes," Kara said.

Finn bolted around the island, dropping to his knees beside the child. He pressed his fingers to her neck. The steady beat reassured him. "Kara, wet a clean towel with some cold water."

"She's stressed, Finn. The poor kid was shook up about meeting you. And it *is* hot in here," Hayden said.

Finn took the towel, laying it across the girl's forehead. After a moment, he wiped her face with it. She had to be Amelia's. The cheekbones were the same…the chestnut hair. Though for all he knew, Amelia's hair color came from a bottle.

"She's sick, idiot! She's got severe aplastic anemia." After Amelia's visit, he'd studied the blood disorder on the Internet, learning how it affected production of the different types of blood cells, making sufferers susceptible to infection, fatigue, bruising and increased bleeding. "She needs a bone marrow transplant."

Kara gasped. "You knew about her?"

"Kinda. Not really." He'd done his best to put it out of his mind, as Amelia had suggested. Fat lot of good that had done. "It's a long story."

"Bone marrow transplant?" Hayden cursed like the former Marine he was.

Knowing what he was thinking, remembering, Finn stole a quick glance at his younger brother. He'd gone as pasty-white as the girl on the floor, raking a hand through his short-cropped hair.

"She's going to be okay, Hayden."

"Yeah. Yeah. Of course she is. You're right."

"She *is*. Her mom's pulling out all the stops for her treatment."

The child's eyes fluttered open, and she tried to sit up. Finn pushed her back. "No, take it easy another minute or two."

"I'm okay."

"You're lying on my kitchen floor. That says otherwise."

The girl's lip trembled and she bit it. That little gesture slammed into his gut. Yeah, Amelia's daughter for sure.

My daughter. Panic constricted his lungs. Two divorces had convinced him family wasn't in his future. He wasn't good at it. And yet...here was his daughter.

Slumped on his kitchen tile.

"Kara, call Elke, ask her to come over here." Their sister Elke was an RN. He'd feel better having someone with actual medical knowledge check her out, reassure him. He scooped the child up and climbed to his feet, waving off Hayden's hovering figure. "Hayden, get the door to the back stairs, will you?" She couldn't weigh much more than his niece, Katie, who was only seven. The girl, *his daughter*—the foreign phrase kept ricocheting around his brain—looped her skinny arms around his neck.

"Where we going?"

"Upstairs. More comfortable than this." At the acrid scent of charring food, Finn realized his entire staff had gathered, all staring at him. "Nobody but me smells that? My food is burning, Marco! Earn your paycheck, will you? Refire that fish. And go easy on the sauces when you plate them. They're not supposed to be swimming when they're served. All of you, get back to work! We have customers to feed!"

Snapped from their train-wreck trances, they scurried in five directions.

Finn climbed the stairs, his brother two steps ahead of him with a backpack slung over his shoulder. "Open up that flower room right next to mine."

"This...this isn't how I imagined meeting you," the girl murmured.

Finn gave her a wry smile. "It's not how I imagined meeting you, either."

"You—*you* imagined meeting *me?*"

The incredulous note tore at his heart. He didn't want to tell her they'd mostly been nightmares in which his sick child accused him of being responsible for the illness...for failing him. Or her, as the case had turned out to be. "I did. Your mother—Amelia *is* your mother, right?" The idea that he might be faced with two different families his impulsive behavior during culinary school had wrought blew his mind. Couldn't be possible. Could it?

At her nod, he stifled a sigh of relief and continued as he reached the top of the stairs, "Your mother wouldn't tell me if you were a girl or a boy. So I imagined meeting both. But never like this. Hey. What's your name?"

"Jordan," Hayden said, from the bedroom's doorway.

Finn scowled at him, easing the girl to the bed. She scooted into the middle. The metal bed frame squeaked as he sat on the edge of the double mattress. "Your name's Jordan?"

"Yes."

"Jordan what?"

Hayden hooted. "You don't remember her mother's last name? That must have been quite the night, my man. Even I haven't done that."

Jordan bolted upright, indignation firing her eyes—eyes the exact same shade that greeted Finn in the mirror each morning. "It's not his fault. He didn't know my mom. He was our sperm donor."

His brother's mouth gaped. The blabbermouth of the family, rendered speechless.

Finn's face heated, but something in his chest softened. Five minutes into their relationship and she was defending him. "Keep your trap shut, Jabber Jaw. Not one word to anyone, you hear me? I'll grind you into sausage and feed you to stray dogs."

"They'd arrest you for cruelty to animals if you did that." His brother x-ed his heart. "You have my word. But...can I be there when you tell Mom?"

Finn grabbed one of the pillows from the bed and hurled

it. Hayden easily caught it, grinning. Jordan giggled.

Finn returned his attention to her. "Speaking of mothers, does yours know you're here?"

She fidgeted. "Uhhh..."

"That's what I figured." He couldn't see the woman who wouldn't even tell him the gender of *her child* giving the kid permission to meet him—especially without Amelia being present to supervise. "She's got to be out of her mind with worry. We have to call her."

The girl's shoulders slumped. "Do we have to do it now?"

"How long have you been gone?"

"What time is it?"

"Seven thirty-two," Hayden said.

"I left Boston at—"

"Boston? How the hell, uh, heck did you get here from Boston by yourself?"

"It was easy."

Jordan recounted her travel adventures—how she'd managed all of it, including how she'd temporarily redirected her mother's e-mails from TravelEasy to a new Zmail e-mail account Jordan had set up for her.

Finn wanted to high-five her for being so damn clever, and shake some sense into her for the risks she'd taken and the panic he knew Amelia had to be experiencing. "Do you have any idea how dangerous that was?"

"Is this going to be my first father-daughter lecture?" she asked.

"Probably." And hopefully the last. 'Cause he had no idea what he was doing. Nor did he *want* to know what he was doing at this point in his life.

She folded her hands and broke into a broad grin. "Okay. Let me have it."

Hayden chortled, still in the doorway.

"Make yourself useful," Finn told him. "Go see if my kitchen's intact and Marco's not poisoning the customers." He looked at his daughter. "Did you eat dinner?"

"No."

"Hungry?"

"A little."

"Allergic to anything?"

"Tomatoes, if I eat too much."

"Bring her up a bowl of the chicken with wild rice soup and some bread." The kid could stand a few carbs. "What do you want to drink?"

"Root beer?"

"Root beer it is. Move it, Hayden."

Hayden hunched over, dragging his foot. "Will that be all, Master?"

Jordan laughed, then covered her mouth with her hand when Finn shook his head. "Don't encourage him." He glanced back at his brother, whose cat-in-the-cream grin told Finn he was enjoying all this just a little too much. "That'll do, Quasi. Try not to spill on the way back up."

"Yes, Master." Hayden disappeared from the room, boot still scraping behind him.

"Cell phone." Finn held out his hand.

"What makes you think I have one?"

"You're what? Thirteen?" She nodded.

"You've got a cell phone. And I want the call to come from it so your mother answers."

Jordan climbed from the bed, unzipping the pouch on the front of the backpack. She slapped it into his palm and plunked herself on the edge of the bed next to him.

###

Amelia paced the small stretch of carpet in front of the dresser and desk. Pencil poised over a little notebook, the young male officer—who looked like he wasn't much older than Jordan—fired off more questions while his partner, an older woman, eyed her warily.

Whether with suspicion or because at six months pregnant Amelia already looked ready to pop, she couldn't decide.

"What was she wearing?"

"I'm not sure. Jeans, sneakers. She was still in her pajamas this morning when I headed down to the conference."

"And you expected to join her for dinner?"

"Yes. She was supposed to order room service for lunch. She wasn't supposed to leave the room at all without me. She's *sick*." They'd already been over this.

"What did she take with her?"

"Her backpack with her laptop, video camera and cell phone."

"Sounds like standard stuff a teenager would want with her while she explores the city," the lady cop said. "Or runs away. You're sure she didn't run?"

Amelia shook her head. "She's not the runaway type. I've never had any problems with Jordan."

"Are there any custody issues?"

"No. She's mine alone."

"No baby-daddy in the picture?" asked the rookie.

Why did everyone always want to know about Jordan's father? It wasn't the dark ages. Single moms were common. "No."

Amelia's cell phone vibrated, then launched into "Sweet Child o' Mine," dancing on the desktop. "That's her now." She lunged for the phone. "Jordan? Where are y—"

"Amelia?" said a male voice on the other end.

As if an arctic breeze had blown into the room, cold raced through her body. "Who is this? Why do you have my daughter's cell phone? What's going on?"

"Relax, Amelia. Everything's fine. Jordan's fine."

"*Who* the hell *is* this?"

The cops watched her intently.

"Finn Hawkins. Jordan is here with me."

Amelia sank into the chair at the desk. "With you? In Erie?"

"Yep. Apparently she's quite resourceful. Smart."

Amelia drew in a deep breath, blowing it out slowly. The baby kicked her hard in the ribs, and she winced, rubbing her rounded belly.

"Everything okay, Dr. Young?" the woman officer asked.

"Hold on." Amelia stabbed the mute button. "Yes, Officers. Thank you very much. My daughter is safe, with, um, a friend." She wasn't going to give the male cop the satisfaction of knowing that her daughter was with her... Amelia mentally choked on the term "baby-daddy." "At least, until I get my hands on her. She's grounded for life after this."

After taking down the details of exactly where Jordan was—needed for their report, they said—the male cop stuffed the notebook into his pocket while his partner nodded sagely.

"I've got two of my own, so I understand. Glad she's safe." The pair headed for the door, the woman speaking into the radio mic clipped to her shoulder.

Amelia unmuted the phone. "Put my daughter on, Mr. Hawkins."

"Mr. Hawkins? I thought we were beyond that, Amelia."

The sexy baritone thrum of his voice made her remember that day in his kitchen.

She clung to her anger at Jordan, the mind-numbing fear she'd experienced moments earlier. "I'm in no mood to play games with you right now. How long will it take me to drive from Boston to your place?"

"Drive? It would be easier to catch a flight. That's what Jordan did."

Another week's grounding—from everything!—got added to Jordan's life sentence. "We drove to Boston, so my car is here."

"Drove to Boston from where?"

"None of your business," she snapped. "How long?"

"I don't know. Long. Eight hours?"

"I'll get on the road now. I'll be there as soon—"

"It's late, Amelia. Why don't you get a good night's rest and start out in the morning?"

"And why don't you put my daughter on the phone, so I can get the yelling out of my system?" Amelia shoved her fist into her lower right lat. The baby squirmed and rolled, a gymnast on speed, thanks to the adrenaline coursing through her system.

"She's eating at the moment. She, uh, she was hungry. Hold on a sec, okay?"

Jordan breathed into the receiver. Amelia sank to the edge of the bed. "Jordan? I can tell it's you."

"Are you mad?"

"Mad doesn't begin to cover it."

"I'm grounded, aren't I?"

"That's a safe bet. Count on other punishment as well."

Jordan sighed. "Don't care. It was worth it."

"I'll be leaving shortly to come get you. We'll discuss it more then. Put—" she fumbled for the right way to refer to him "—Mr. Hawkins back on."

"Just a minute."

In the background, Amelia heard him speaking to someone else. "Thanks, Hayden. Yeah, I'll be down in a few minutes. Tell Marco he's not to even attempt the risotto for table ten. Basic dish, but somehow he wrecks it every time. Jordan, I'm going to talk to your mom in the hallway for now, okay?"

"Okay." Her daughter's voice, even from a distance, was music to Amelia's ears.

The idea of losing her, in any way... Amelia's nose tingled, and she bit down on her lower lip. There would be no crying. Jordan was safe. *Damn hormones.*

She stalked to the closet, yanking clothes from the hangers with one hand and tossing them into the open suitcase on the stand.

"Amelia? Look, take your time getting here. Be safe. We'll...well...we'll manage to take care of her. I have three unoccupied bedrooms here, and she can have her pick. I'm certainly capable of feeding her. And not pizza or junk food. You've got nothing to worry about."

Nothing to worry about except for her vulnerable daughter bonding with a man she was never going to see again.

"She's not your daughter," she reminded him, bending over to pull Jordan's pink eyelet socks from the bottom dresser drawer. "She's mine. I don't want her hurt because she wants more than you can give her."

"Seems to me she's already been hurt because she wants more than *you* can give her, Amelia. Like a father."

She straightened up so fast the baby jolted her with another shot to the ribs. The kid, whether male or female, she didn't know—she was saving that as the one surprise of the whole process—was going to be a hockey player. After unclenching her teeth, Amelia muttered, "Plenty of kids grow up without a father."

"And isn't that a shame? I guess when I originally donated my sperm I was thinking more along the lines of married couples who couldn't have children. I didn't envision children growing up without a father."

She wanted to cram Finn Hawkins's arrogant self-righteousness down his throat. He'd known her daughter all of two minutes, and already he was lecturing *her* on the importance of fathers?

Finn's voice softened as he added, "She just wanted to know me, Amelia. To know something more about herself in the process. And I'm going to spend every second between now and when you get here making that happen."

All the energy and strength drained out of her as she stared at the now-silent phone.

Words failed her. But then, there was no one to hear a snappy comeback even if she had one.

Jordan.

And Finn Hawkins. Together.

The very thought raised goose bumps on her arms.

The man had played his part in Amelia's life. In her plan. And now he needed to stay out of it.

CHAPTER FOUR

A DISQUIETING SENSE OF déjà vu settled around Amelia as she turned into the parking lot of Finn's restaurant-home, empty except for two vehicles. There had been many changes in eight months. No more construction equipment, for one. And the trees were now green.

Get in, get what you came for, get out, she reminded herself. *Just like last time.*

Her face warmed. Okay, maybe not *just* like that. Last time she'd gotten way more than she'd bargained for from him.

She slid from her Liberty, taking a moment to stretch out the travel kinks. She'd driven several hours the night before, until exhaustion had forced her to find a motel.

It had galled her when she'd called her daughter's cell and gotten Finn instead, who reported that Jordan was sleeping peacefully in one of his guest bedrooms.

Now almost eleven in the morning, Amelia headed, as instructed, toward the back entrance of the place. Apparently Fresh didn't serve Sunday brunch or Sunday anything, for that matter.

She hurried past the padlocked silver walk-in freezer at the edge of the parking lot and down the sidewalk, entering the covered porch at the rear of the building. As she reached for the doorknob, the view through the window brought her up short.

Jordan and Finn stood at the work island. Her daughter beamed at the man as she scraped something from a bowl into a pan.

Jordan hadn't looked that happy, that enthusiastic, since before her diagnosis.

Amelia's hand trembled. Was it right to keep Jordan from getting to know him?

She squared her shoulders. Damn skippy it was. Without so much as a knock, she walked into the kitchen. Her daughter slid the pan into one of the wall ovens.

Two pairs of identical aquamarine eyes turned toward her.

"Mom! Check this out! We're making..."

Amelia's you-are-in-so-much-trouble-young-lady-and-just-wait-till-I-get-you-out-of-here scowl wilted Jordan's smile. The girl studied her sneakers.

Finn patted her shoulder.

Amelia's stomach tightened at the familiar and slightly possessive gesture. "Get your things, Jordan. It's almost a sixteen-hour drive home. I want to be back on the road in five minutes."

Jordan's head snapped up. "But Mom—"

"Don't *but Mom* me. You scared me almost to death. You went on a plane, for crying out loud. Do you have any idea how many germs are in the air on a plane? Your counts have been good, but you know how fast that can change. What the hell were you thinking?"

Anger simmered in her daughter's eyes and Jordan propped her fists on her hips. "I wanted to meet my father. You wouldn't let me. I found a way. You always tell me we've got to have a plan. I made a plan. Who needs Make-a-Wish?"

"Don't talk to me like that. Your wish is fulfilled. You've met him. Now we're leaving. I'm not going to say it again. Get your stuff and let's go."

"Amelia," Finn began.

She jabbed a finger in his direction. "You be quiet. You have zero say here, so keep your opinions to yourself."

His eyebrows climbed his forehead. He gave Jordan's shoulder another pat and nodded down at her. "Go on. Run upstairs and grab your backpack."

Amelia's molars threatened to crack as she clamped her jaw together.

"But the triple chocolate brownies..." her daughter protested.

"I'll box them up and send them to you tomorrow. Overnight. They'll be at your house by Tuesday."

"But I wanted to meet everyone! You said—"

"What I said doesn't matter. I'm sorry you can't stay for Sunday dinner and meet more of the family. But you have to obey your mom."

"Whatever." With a sullen look cast in Amelia's direction, Jordan crossed the kitchen, stabbed a code into the keypad, then yanked the door to the back staircase so hard it slammed into the wall and bounced closed behind her. Her feet pounded up the steps.

Finn folded his arms.

Amelia did the same.

For a long moment, they simply stared each other down across his kitchen. Then he tilted his head slightly. "Great to see you again, Dr. Amelia Young of Caribou, Maine." He put a touch of accent on her last name and home town.

Amelia cursed Jordan's big mouth and easy trust. "Use that information to contact us, and I will slap a restraining order on you so fast you won't know what hit you."

He threw his hands in the air. "For God's sake, Amelia. What kind of bogeyman do you think I am? Do I look like a serial killer or something? What could be so horrible about *your* daughter getting to know me? Having contact with me?"

"We don't need you. We're perfectly fine by ourselves, the way we've always been."

Finn struggled to keep his gaze from sliding down to her rounded belly. The moment she'd barged into his kitchen, he'd wrestled with the impulse to stare. The changes pregnancy had brought...well, it wasn't so much that she had the "glow" his sisters sometimes talked about. The glow his sister Elke was showing in her first pregnancy. No, Amelia's body was more...lush. Ripening.

Hot. And despite the fact that she was making him crazy with her behavior, the desire to take her in his arms again, to kiss her... Finn understood the temptation Adam must have felt when he'd been offered the apple. He knew he shouldn't even *want* it, let alone *have* it, and yet...

His child—his *second* child—grew in that lovely, curvy stomach. A child he'd never know, just like Jordan. Which, given his track record with family-building of his own, might be for the best. "I'm glad I had the chance to meet her. She's a great kid, Amelia."

The furrows between her eyebrows softened. "Most of the time she is."

"Will you think about letting her keep in touch with me? I

want to know how this all turns out."

Amelia shook her head. "There's nothing to think about. You are a sperm donor. Nothing more. You gave up any rights when you signed the piece of paper at the clinic."

He curled his fingers into his palms. He wasn't asking to be a father. Just to be kept in the damn loop.

He was struck by a flash of insight. The legal eagles in the family—his father, oldest brother, Alan, sister Cathy, and baby brother Kyle, though the squirt had yet to finish law school and pass the bar—would be proud. Finn smiled a slow, wolfish grin. He knew just how to wipe that smug look off her face. "I didn't sign any papers this time. Guess you forgot that step, huh?"

Amelia's eyes widened. The color blanched from her face and she swayed.

He took two quick steps in her direction before she held up her hand. "I'm fine. Where's the bathroom, before I hit the road?"

"Out the kitchen, first door on the right." He pointed.

She casually sauntered from the room, but her footsteps on the other side of the swinging door gave away her haste.

Finn gathered up the brownie dishes, a twinge—but only a twinge—of guilt pricking him for shaking her up like that. Let her sweat over the fact that he might have a claim to Baby Number Two. Even if he didn't intend to exercise that claim.

Finn didn't have what it took to take care of someone, not even a wife, never mind children. His second divorce had driven the point home. One failed marriage could have been a fluke. Just a mistake. But two?

Knowing Jordan had been temporary from the second

she'd keeled over in his kitchen made this easier.

He had the area clean when Jordan, backpack slung over both shoulders and followed by Hayden, dejectedly slumped from the staircase.

"Where's my mom?" she asked, scanning the room.

"Bathroom."

"Figures."

Hayden crossed his arms and leaned against the wall, a somber expression on his face. Because Jordan's situation so closely mirrored Ian's, Hayden had taken an immediate shine to her.

The kid grabbed both straps of her pack, crossed to Finn, then thrust out her right hand. "It's been great. I'm glad I had a chance to meet you."

A lump swelled in Finn's throat. They'd spent the morning cooking, swapping stories...bonding. She'd made videos of the restaurant and his cooking lesson. It had been fun. Of course, it was easy to play at being a dad for a few hours. He leaned over and pulled her into his arms, backpack and all. His first attempt to speak derailed into clearing his throat. "Me, too. Good luck, kiddo."

She burrowed her face in the crook of his neck, sniffling softly.

He tightened his grip. Her tiny frame felt vulnerable in his embrace.

"I—I memorized your phone number," she whispered. "I don't dare put it in my cell. Can I call you sometime?"

Torn between Amelia's wishes and his own surprising desire to keep in touch, he murmured, "Don't get caught."

That evoked a sharp chuckle-snort. "No kidding."

###

Amelia paused at the swinging door, uncertain, running her shaking hand over her baby bump. The rational part of her kept saying it was probably nothing. There hadn't been much blood, only a little spotting. The rest of her screamed in terror.

Two lives rode on this pregnancy.

And she was hundreds of miles from her OB, had no idea where the nearest hospital was and didn't want to transmit her fear to her daughter.

She took several deep breaths, then pushed through the door.

As she entered the kitchen, Jordan untangled herself from Finn's embrace, wiping beneath her eyes.

Amelia's heart lurched.

"I'm ready, Mom."

"Thanks, honey." Her voice sounded strained even to herself.

Another man—one of his brothers, she'd guess, given the similar jawline—lounged against the wall. Amelia jerked her head toward the door. Working harder to keep her tone steady, she said, "You mind if I have a word with you in private?"

"Why not?" Finn strode toward her. "If I'm not back when the timer goes off, pull those brownies, huh?" he said to the presumed brother.

"Do I get to eat them?"

"No. They're Jordan's."

"I'll share," her daughter said.

Amelia followed Finn into the hallway.

"What's up?" he asked as soon as the door closed behind them. "More threats about restraining orders? Did you whip up some legal papers for me to sign while you were in the john?"

"No." She sighed. "Forget it. I'll figure it out myself, as usual. Google knows everything. I'll just ask it."

He grabbed her by the arm before she could pass him. Heat spiraled from his fingers into her flesh. Finn Hawkins was entirely too sexy for her own good. The narrow walls of the hallway created an intimate, cozy atmosphere, and once more she cursed the pregnancy hormones. "Let go of me."

He did. Immediately. The flush in his sculpted cheekbones said he'd felt the heat, too.

One more reason to get the hell out of Erie and never look back.

"I'm sorry," he said. "What did you want?"

"It's nothing. Never mind."

"Amelia."

She glanced up, finding genuine concern in his eyes.

"If you or Jordan need anything...I want to help. So what is it?"

A few moments of his frank stare ratcheted up her fear again, and made her confess. "I—I'm spotting."

"Spotting?" His gaze traveled her face, her arms. "Hives?"

"Uh, no." She gestured at her stomach, and vaguely lower. "Spotting." Her voice trembled again. "The baby? It's probably nothing but..."

"Oh. *Spotting*. Oh, crap!" He fumbled in his pocket, withdrawing his cell phone, stabbing a button.

"Wait! What are you doing?"

"Calling a doctor."

"I need an ob-gyn."

"I'm not an idiot."

"You have an ob-gyn on speed dial?"

"She's my sister, and she's one of the best in Erie."

"I didn't ask you to call anyone. Especially not your sister." The last thing she needed was another "family" member to find out about Jordan. And the new baby. God only knew how many Hawkinses Jordan had already met. Fortunately, Amelia had made it to Erie before the family dinner Finn had mentioned earlier. Online articles about him had mentioned his large family, with siblings named from A to a pair of twins with K names. Which made Finn number six in the series of twelve. "I wanted to know if there was an urgent care nearby. It's probably nothing." If she said it enough times, perhaps it would be so. And she'd feel foolish about making a big deal over it. *Please, please, please, let it be so.*

His eyebrows drew together. "You're going to get *urgent care.* And with a sixteen-hour drive ahead of you, you can't afford to assume it's nothing. Let's err on the side of caution, okay?" The ring coming from the phone stopped, and was replaced by a faint female voice.

"Bethany? I need help. I have a, uh, an out-of-town friend here. She's pregnant, and she's spotting. It's Sunday. And you're the best." He paused, shaking his head. "I'm not sure. Hold on." He jabbed another button on the cell and held it out. "You're on speakerphone. Go ahead."

"How far along are you?" asked his sister, the doctor.

"Twenty-six weeks."

"Okay. Any history of problems?"

"No."

"Any previous spotting?"

"No."

"Are you high-risk at all?"

"Well...I'm in my forties."

The woman on the phone chuckled. "Yeah, me, too. You've gotta love being referred to as 'advanced maternal age,' don't you?"

"I wanted to slap my ob-gyn when he mentioned it."

"My kind of girl. Look, it's probably nothing."

The muscles in Amelia's shoulders unknotted. "That's what I said."

Finn yanked the phone back, spoke directly into it. "She has a sixteen-hour drive home, Bethany. I'm not letting her start a trip like that without knowing for sure that it's nothing."

"Take a pill, Finnegan Beginagain. I didn't say I wouldn't see her. I'm almost to Mom and Dad's. Let me drop the kids off for Sunday dinner, and I'll meet you at my office. Twenty minutes."

The connection broke before Amelia could protest. Thus preserving some of her energy for the arguments she found herself in two minutes later, with both Finn and Jordan.

"You're not coming," she said. "Either of you." Hospitals and doctor's offices teemed with germs and bacteria. Given that Jordan didn't produce enough white blood cells, the body's defense system, infection and illness were serious threats. Besides, she spent enough time in medical surroundings.

"*I'm* coming," Finn retorted. "You don't know where the office is, and I'm not telling you. You shouldn't be driving. Take it easy and let me handle this."

"I'm coming, too," Jordan insisted. "What if you need me? And I can't stay here by myself."

Finn's brother, now wearing a blue oven mitt and juggling the pan of hot brownies out of the oven, cleared his throat. "What am I, chopped liver? I'm here. You're not going to be alone, pip."

"Exactly," Finn said. "Hayden will take care of Jordan. Trust me, he's got plenty of babysitting experience."

"I'm not a baby," Jordan said. "I don't need sitting."

Amelia fought the urge to clap her hands over her ears. "Enough. You—" she pointed at her daughter "—are staying here. You wanted more time? Be careful what you wish for. Get Finn's brother to tell you more about their family. Because as soon as I'm done at the doctor's, we're out of here. And since you're grounded for life, you won't be coming back." She veered her finger toward Finn. "Let's go."

On the way out she muttered, "But if you think you're going anywhere near that exam room, buddy, have I got news for you."

The multistory brick building that housed the group office Bethany shared with several other ob-gyns connected to St. Joseph's Hospital via an enclosed walkway on the third floor. The proximity reassured Finn as he drove under it, then turned into the parking lot.

The fact that Bethany waited on the sidewalk with Elke was far less reassuring.

Finn stifled a groan. Elke knew all about Jordan. He'd called her for medical advice last night.

"What's wrong?" Amelia asked.

"The one on the left is Bethany. The doctor. The pregnant one is my sister Elke. She's an RN. We call her the Interrogator, so brace yourself. She came out last night to check on Jordan."

"Check on her why?"

"She, uh..." He hated to give Amelia anything else to worry about right now. "She got a bit light-headed in the heat of the kitchen last night. I figured, given her medical situation, it would be a good idea for Elke to take a look at her."

"And you're only telling me this now?" Anger brought more color back to her face, reassuring him.

"Umm..."

Bethany saved him by opening the passenger-side door to his Explorer. "Hi. I'm Dr. Hawkins. Good to meet you, though not under these circumstances." Bethany offered Amelia a hand out of the car, which she accepted.

"Dr. Amelia Young. Likewise."

"Oh? You're a doctor, too?" Bethany beamed in approval. "What's your specialty?"

"I'm a chiropractor. I know, most MDs think that means I'm not a real doctor."

"I'm not one of them," Bethany said. "There have been times I wouldn't have been able to move without mine. I brought Elke with me. She's an RN. I thought having someone else present would make you feel more comfortable. But that's entirely up to you."

"A doctor, a nurse... Quite the talented family you have, Finn." Amelia's expression said she'd made a fine choice in DNA for her kids.

She made him feel like a slab of meat. *Fill this cup, Finn. Give me your genes, Finn. I'll pay you, Finn. But don't come near this child, or else...* "Don't forget the *lawyers*. We've got a handful of those in the gene pool, too."

Her mouth gaped. She snapped it shut. They entered the building while Elke introduced herself, then slid into the smooth chatter she used to disarm all her interrogation subjects. "So," she said as the elevator doors shut. "You're the mother of Finn's secret love child. Jordan's a great kid—"

"Elke!" Bethany snapped. "Professional, I said. Not personal. You're here to assist me as a nurse. Not to grill her."

"Love child?" Amelia shook her head. "Love had nothing to do with it."

"What?" Elke tipped her head to the side. "That doesn't sound like my brother. Not this one, anyway. How did you guys meet?"

Finn had left out a lot of details in what he'd told Elke last night, explaining as little as possible despite his sister's attempts to wheedle more information. "We *connected* while I was in culinary school," he said now. Not exactly a lie. But not precisely true, either.

He scowled at Amelia, hoping to shut her up about the sperm donation.

"Connected." Amelia's mouth pursed. "Yes, I suppose we did."

"Finn told me about Jordan's severe aplastic anemia. I'm

so sorry." Elke gestured toward Amelia's middle. "So...interesting that you're expecting again."

Don't rise to the bait, don't rise to the bait.... Finn hoped Amelia could read his mind.

"Your brother mentioned you checked Jordan out last night. Something about overheating in the kitchen? She wasn't running a fever, was she?"

"No, no fever. She was tired, hungry and nervous about meeting Finn." Elke narrowed her eyes.

"Elke," he warned. "Whatever you're about to ask, it's none of your business. Put a sock in it."

"Okay. How about I ask you a few questions then?"

"No." He folded his arms.

"Is this your baby, too?"

He pointedly ignored her. The elevator slid to a stop with a *ding,* and the doors opened.

His sisters exchanged a glance as they exited.

Bethany unlocked the office, flipping on the lights. "You wait here, Finn." She turned to Amelia. "Do you want Elke in with us?

Amelia nodded. "That's fine."

"Why do I have to wait out here? Why can't I wait outside the exam room?" Finn struggled not to sound like a petulant child, but didn't quite pull it off.

"Because we spent a lot of money decorating this room so people could *wait* in it. It's why we call it a waiting room." Bethany escorted Amelia and Elke through another door, out of his sight.

The tables held pamphlets about various birth control methods and STDs. The magazines mostly boasted pictures of big-bellied women or babies on the covers. Finn prowled the seating area in desperate search of a *Sports Illustrated* or even a news magazine. He'd give his sister a lecture on prospective fathers' rights to decent reading material later at their parents' house.

Fathers' rights. At the moment, that phrase seemed oxymoronic, and left a bitter taste in his mouth. Or maybe that was from the unexpected fear he'd felt since Amelia had mentioned the spotting.

The tightly closed door to the inner offices taunted him.

He resisted. Briefly. Then he quietly slipped through, into the maze of corridors. If there was anything going on with the baby, he wanted to know about it. As the father, it *was* his *right*. And Amelia wasn't likely to tell him.

He crept down the carpeted hallway, head tipped to the side, listening intently. The low murmur of voices gave away their location in exam room 6.

But it didn't give away anything else. Finn paced, his black chef's clogs creating scuff lines in the nap of the beige rug.

"Oh, crap!" Bethany exclaimed clearly a few minutes later. "No, no! Don't move! Stay lying down! Elke, get the head down on this table. All the way."

Finn darted to the door. On the other side, a whirring noise competed with his sister's continued admonitions that Amelia stay still. As he reached for the handle, Bethany burst out. Without so much as a glare at him, she raced to the administration desk in the middle of the hall, grabbing the phone.

Heart pounding, Finn peeked into the exam room. Amelia, the lower part of her body covered with a white sheet, lay on her back. The exam table tilted at an extreme angle, with her head down. Elke stood at her side, murmuring calming words he couldn't make out.

He scrambled after his sister.

"This is Dr. Hawkins," she barked into the phone. "I need a gurney at my office to transfer a patient into the hospital, and I need it *now*. Get me an LDRP room."

"What's going on?" Finn asked. What the hell was an LDRP room?

Bethany held up a hand while she repeated her demands, then hung up the phone. She strode back to the exam room, Finn on her heels. Just before they reached it, he grabbed her by the arm. "Beth! Tell me what's happening. 'Oh crap' isn't something I imagine you usually say to a patient."

"Finn, I can't—"

He squeezed gently. "It's *my* baby. That baby *is* a Hawkins. And my thirteen-year-old daughter's life depends on this baby."

Bethany's eyes grew wider. Bewilderment gave way to sympathy. "I wondered if it was a savior sibling. I'll do my best, Finn." She shook her head. "But it's not good. Come on. I'll explain it to you both."

Amelia lifted her head when he followed his sister into the exam room. She tugged at the sheet covering her body. "I don't want him in here—"

"Keep your head down, Amelia. I mean it. Don't move. This is important, so lie still and listen. You have an incompetent cervix. That means it's opening already, without contractions. When I examined you, I felt a foot."

Elke stroked Amelia's shoulder.

Amelia sucked in a deep breath, face blanching the color of the sheet—no easy feat given that her head pointed toward the floor. "The baby's coming now?"

"Not if I can help it. The sac is still intact. What I want to do is called cervical cerclage. I'm going to sew your cervix shut to keep that baby inside, where he belongs. Though at twenty-six weeks, there's about an eighty percent rate of survival, there can also be a lot of complications for the baby. Why risk it if we don't have to?"

"If—if it doesn't work, and the baby comes now, will there be enough cord blood to transplant into Jordan?"

Bethany shook her head. "I'm not certain, but I doubt it. The size of the baby relates to the volume of cord blood."

Finn's heart pounded against his ribs. Sweat beaded across his forehead. If she lost this child, then Jordan...

"We need to keep you tilted like this for a while and let gravity pull the baby farther into the uterus. I'll be monitoring you for any contractions for several hours, too. Once an ultrasound confirms that the baby is back where we need him to be, I'll move you to an OR and stitch your cervix."

"Dr. Hawkins?" a man called from the hallway.

Bethany popped her head out the door. "Down here. Hurry up."

Finn automatically reached for Amelia's hand. She stared up at him, tears welling in her eyes, teeth pinching her lower lip. For a moment her fingers lay limp in his. Then she squeezed so hard she could have cracked a walnut.

"Don't tell Jordan yet. I don't want her worrying needlessly."

"Don't worry about Jordan. I...we'll take care of her. This

family takes care of its own. And like it or not, she's family."

CHAPTER FIVE

SEVERAL AGONIZING HOURS ticked by, broken by Elke's occasional visits to the labor and delivery family waiting room—where Finn had been exiled because Amelia wouldn't let him be with her—to provide updates. The Hawkins family grapevine hadn't taken long to kick in, especially as Finn himself had contacted Greg, and now several of his family waited with him. The Hawkinses *did* take care of their own.

In one of the chairs that dotted the perimeter, Kara focused on the screen of an ebook reader, glancing at him every time he strode past. Derek and Greg, undoubtedly bored out of their minds, sprawled on one of the back-to-back, blindingly yellow couches that occupied the middle of the room, leaving a wide pathway to pace between them and the chairs.

Finn circled the room again. As he rounded the sofa's corner, Greg stretched out a leg, blocking him.

"Sit down for two seconds, would you? You're making everyone in here more stressed."

"If it were Shannon in there, would you be sitting down?"

"That's different. I love—"

"Pretend it's a year ago. You barely know her." Greg and Shannon's wedding was in a few weeks. "Pretend she's pregnant with your kid, to save the life of your *other* kid, and you don't know what's going on."

Derek, a widower with three kids of his own, elbowed Greg. "Leave him alone. One of these days you'll understand. Pregnancy makes men crazy, too." He grabbed Greg's jeans, pulled his leg out of the way. "Pace away, fish."

Greg glanced past Finn and grimaced. "Uh-oh. Brace yourself. Mom just walked through the door, and judging by the look on her face, your ass is grass, man."

Finn turned as his mother stormed into the room. He drew a deep breath.

"I figured I'd find you boys here with him. Kara, I didn't expect you were in on this."

Kara's lips moved in protest, but before she could form a coherent word, their mom held up her hand. "Why do you even try to keep stuff from me? Two of my daughters, my daughters with medical skills, both ditched Sunday dinner before it got started. Two of my sons didn't even show up. Two more of my sons, after receiving numerous text messages—" his mother glared at Derek and Greg. She hated cell phone usage during meals "—ran out like the house was on fire as soon as the meal was over. Leaving all the children for Shannon to deal with, I might add."

"Mom, I—" Finn began.

But his mother shook her head. "Finnegan Rand Hawkins, what were you thinking? A sperm donor?"

Heat flushed his face. He cleared his throat. "Obviously, you've heard the whole story, then."

"Don't blame Hayden. He did his best. He wouldn't answer his cell phone, or the phone at the restaurant. So I went over there. I've already met my granddaughter. What Hayden didn't spill, Jordan did. That poor child is frantic about her mother and the baby. What she's not saying is how scared she is about herself."

Finn puffed up his cheeks, blew out the air.

"A bone marrow transplant." His mother's voice quavered. Her blue eyes watered.

Finn pulled her into a bear hug. "So you understand why I agreed to a second child with Amelia, right?"

She nodded against his shoulder. "I do."

"Then I'm forgiven?"

"I didn't say that." She broke away from his embrace. "What you did has serious repercussions, Finn."

Understatement of the year. "Obviously, Mom. Can we save that lecture for later?" *Perhaps years later? Maybe for Jordan's college graduation?* "Where's Dad?"

"Your father decided to stop in the chapel downstairs. He'll be up shortly."

That drove the seriousness of the situation home for Finn. That Michael Hawkins, a man of quiet faith, had decided it warranted a visit to the chapel...

Finn sank to the edge of a chair, leaned forward and propped his elbows on his knees. The heels of his palms pressed against his cheekbones as he covered his face.

Any minute now he would wake up to discover that the past twenty-four hours, from meeting Jordan, to teaching her how to bake brownies the way his nanna had taught him, to this very moment when the fate of both children hung in the balance, had been just another of his who-is-my-child nightmares.

Any minute now...

His mother eased down beside him, rubbing his back.

The room grew quieter. The weight of his siblings' stares made the hair on his neck prickle.

From the direction of the doorway, someone cleared a throat. "Finn?"

Bethany. He rubbed his face, then scrambled to his feet. "What?"

At some point she'd donned a white doctor coat over her jeans and soft pink shirt, adding to her air of authority. Adrenaline coursed through him. He wiped his palms across his pants.

His sister jerked her head toward the hall. "A word with you?"

Shithelldamn. What could she possibly want that she couldn't—or wouldn't—say in front of the family?

"Be right back," he told them as he hustled out the door. He followed her a few steps down the corridor before she turned to face him.

"Everything that can go right at the moment is. Gravity has worked in our favor, and the baby has moved back down into the uterus, away from the cervix."

Finn's legs trembled with relief. "You couldn't say that in there? You scared me to death with the top secret stuff."

"I'm not supposed to be talking to you about it at all, Finn. Privacy laws?"

"I'm the *father,* damn it."

"As long as that baby stays inside, where we want him, you have no rights at all. It's her body, her choices, and you've got no say."

"If he'd been born a few hours ago, and was in the baby intensive care unit—"

"NICU."

"Whatever. Then I'd have a say?"

"Yep."

"That sucks."

"Life often does." Bethany reached into the pocket of her coat. "But since I'm flouting the rules for you, Beginagain, I figured I'd go all the way." She pulled out several small pieces of white paper. "Ultrasound pictures. It's a boy."

"A boy?" He accepted the glossy sheets from her, turned them in several directions.

Bethany reached over, putting them right side up, and pointed. "Here's the proof, right here. These are his legs, and this is...well, you know what it is."

At her fingertip, he could make out two smallish blobs and one larger one. A boy. Amelia carried his son.

Warmth spread across Finn's chest. Followed quickly by a constriction around his ribs that made it hard to breathe.

"I'm taking her into the OR in a few minutes."

That didn't help. He shoved the ultrasound pictures in his pocket. "What are the risks?"

"Plenty. Including the fact that I could accidentally nick the amniotic sac."

"That would be bad?"

"That would be very bad."

His stomach knotted. "Okay. Don't do that."

"I don't plan to."

"Good." Finn took her arm. "Thanks, Bethy. For everything."

"Don't thank me yet. This is only the first step, and the odds aren't in our favor. But I'm going to do my best." She gave him a quick hug. "I'll send word when she's in recovery."

"Wait." He pulled her back. "Can I see her before you take her in?"

His sister shook her head sympathetically. "I'm sorry, Finn. She's made it very clear that you're not allowed in there. That's one highly independent woman. She reminds me a little bit of Shannon."

"How so?"

"Keeping everyone at arm's length." Bethany sighed. "This is going to be really hard on her. A princess who expects people to wait on her hand and foot would have a much easier time." She patted his elbow. "I have to go. I'll keep you in the loop."

He watched her stride down the hallway, calm, confident. In control.

He'd give anything to feel the same way. He'd never felt more helpless in his life, not even when Marianna, his second wife, had filed for divorce. He wanted to do something, anything, to tip the odds in their favor. No wonder Amelia had been so driven to have this second child, to take action of her own to save Jordan's life.

Waiting around, doing nothing, sucked.

Amelia struggled to stay wrapped in the soothing fog of the medication they'd given her. No worries here. No stress. Just peaceful, blissful nothingness.

Vaguely, she remembered being told the operation had gone well. Being returned to the pretty labor and delivery room from the surgical recovery room.

At least she thought she remembered. Maybe she'd made it all up?

The whoosh of the fetal monitor indicated the baby's heartbeat was strong and fast. Reassured, she let the medication pull her back into sleep.

The next time she surfaced, a man's voice, low but animated, overpowered the sounds of the monitor.

"...look, kid..." A pause. "Dill. I'm not going to be around much. And given my track record, that could be for the best. But since I'm not going to be around to tell you what to do in the future, I want you to listen to me now. As your father—"

Father? Still loath to wake up completely, Amelia cracked open one eye. Finn sat in a chair at the side of her bed, leaning over her stomach.

Her still nicely rounded stomach.

"—I'm telling you, stay in your room." He laughed softly. "You've got an important job, Dill. You're a hero before you're even here. Your sister is counting on you. It's not really fair, but then, so much in life isn't. Hard truth to learn before you're even born. And some people would think it's a horrible thing, bringing you into the world to save your sister's life. I don't know your mother all that well, but I can tell you this— she loves your sister like crazy, and I can't help but think that means she's going to love you just as much. Maybe even more. But we won't tell Jordan that because it would hurt her feelings."

Amelia's nose tingled.

Even some parents of other kids waiting for a BMT had taken her to task for "playing God" and having another child specifically to save Jordan.

How could she not do everything in her power to save her? She was Jordan's mother. It was her duty to do anything and everything she could...because the idea of losing her was too much to bear.

And the fact that Finn knew how much she already loved this new baby... She sniffled.

He jerked his gaze to her face. "Hey. You're awake? Oh, now, don't cry. It's okay." He reached over to the bedside table, pulled out a tissue and pressed it into her hand. "Dill is doing great. Everything went well."

"D-dill?" She dabbed at her eyes. It had to be the shock of the surgery, the remnants of the medication, making her so unsteady. So emotional. She struggled to swallow the lump. No crying. Especially not in front of Finn.

She'd show no weakness to the man who, only hours ago, had threatened, however veiled, to fight for the child she carried.

He grinned. "Yeah, Dill. I didn't want to keep calling him *kid.*"

"Him?" Clarity began to dawn. She crushed the tissue in her hand. "Him?"

Finn's grin got larger and his eyes twinkled. "Yeah. It's a boy."

"Arggh." She tossed the tissue at him. It bounced off his ear and onto the floor. "I didn't want to know that! It was supposed to be a surprise."

"Oh." The spark faded from his eyes, and the dimple on the right side of his mouth vanished, calling attention to the five o'clock shadow that stubbled his jaw. "Sorry. I didn't realize that."

She sighed. "Too late now. But why Dill?"

One corner of his mouth twitched. "Well...a food nick-name sorta came natural to me. Dill pickle? You're pregnant. What do pregnant women crave?"

"Ah. Okay. Except I don't crave dill pickles."

"What do you crave?"

"Potato chip and marshmallow fluff sandwiches on white bread."

He wrinkled his nose. "Lovely combo. But potato doesn't have the same ring as Dill. Can't call a boy Fluff, either. He'll be scarred for life before he's born. Chip?"

Someone rapped on the door, and Dr. Hawkins called out, "Amelia?" His sister scowled when she saw Finn planted in the rocking chair he'd dragged over to the bedside. "You're not supposed to be in here."

"It's okay. He's fine," Amelia said.

The woman looked skeptical.

"Really. He's not bothering me."

Her eyebrows rose. She strode to the fetal monitor to study the flashing display. "The baby looks good right now. Strong heartbeat, you're not having any contractions. I'm pleased to say we made it over the first hurdle."

"The first?" Amelia groped for the controls to the bed. Try-ing to carry on a conversation while lying flat on your back, with people standing next to you, was uncomfortable.

Dr. Hawkins took the rectangular box from her hand just as she found the up button. "No, sorry. You're not allowed to be upright yet. You have to stay absolutely flat for now."

"Ugh. Okay. How long is 'for now'?"

"If everything goes perfectly, I'll remove the stitches about a week before your due date. You can get up for occasional trips to the bathroom, but—"

"A week before my due date?" The shriek in her voice made Finn wince. "That's three months! Please tell me you're joking. And by the way, it's not a funny joke."

"Sorry. If you want to keep that baby in there, you need to keep as little pressure as possible on your cervix. Stitches are great, but not enough if you go running around, carrying on life as normal."

"But...but..." Millions of thoughts, questions, crowded her brain. "I have a practice to maintain."

"You don't have a partner?"

"No. I made arrangements with a colleague in the next town to cover my patients when I have the baby, and when I take Jordan to Portland for the transplant, but..." She looked up at Finn's sister. "My patients and staff are extremely supportive of Jordan and her battle, but my practice might not recover from this much time off."

"Jordan won't recover without the transplant, right? She'll die?"

Amelia blew out a long breath. "Right."

"You've already gone through so much to make her survival possible. You can get through the rest. I'll be keeping you here for another day or two to monitor everything. After that, I'll see you once a week. We'll do an ultrasound at least once a month, more if I think we need to."

"Wait, wait, wait." Amelia pressed her fingertips to her forehead. "What do you mean, *you'll* see me? You said you have to keep me in the hospital only for another day or two. I have an ob-gyn in Maine. You said I have to stay flat on my back, but surely I can get home somehow. Medical transport. Something..."

The doctor shared a look with Finn before stepping closer to the bed. "I wouldn't recommend it. Air transportation is risky because of the changes of pressure. And a sixteen-hour ride in an ambulance?" She shook her head. "I'd highly advise against it. Too much can go wrong too quickly."

"Where the hell do you suggest I stay then, Doctor? You're booting me out of the hospital to where?"

"Finn has tons of room at his place. You and Jordan will stay there, of course. As my brother said, we take care of our own."

Finn's shock no doubt mirrored Amelia's own. His eyes widened. "What?" He shook his head. "No. I don't—I can't... I have a restaurant to run and—"

Dr. Hawkins grabbed his arm, dragging him toward the door. "We'll be right back," she said to Amelia. "A word in the hallway, Finn."

Amelia scrunched her eyes shut, shaking her head.

This wasn't happening.

Finn waited for the door to click closed behind Bethany before unloading on her. "Are you crazy? Telling her they could stay with me? What the hell were you thinking?"

Bethany folded her arms, narrowing her eyes. "Exactly what I just said. What *you* said earlier. The Hawkins family takes care of their own. Don't you want the chance to get to know your daughter?"

"No. Yes." He dragged his hand over his face. "Hell, Bethy.

You've backed me into a corner, haven't you?"

"That woman is carrying your son. You'd hang her out to dry?"

"They could stay at Mom's. She's got plenty of room, too. And she loves to take care of people. Me? I suck at it. Besides, I have a business to run."

Bethany shook her head. "I never took you for a coward, Beginagain. Or the kind of man who abandons a woman carrying his child."

"Hey. That's harsh. I'm not abandoning her. Them. She's the one who keeps insisting they're *not* my kids." He shifted from foot to foot, then pressed his spine against the wall, glancing down at his shoe. The hospital's paging system called for a doctor to report to the nurses' station.

"Jordan's waiting on a bone marrow transplant. What would Ian think?"

His stomach tightened. He jerked his head up. "Low blow, Bethy. You don't fight fair."

She pursed her lips. "No, I don't. Not where my patients are concerned. And right now, Amelia and her baby are my patients. They need you."

He shoved his hands into his pockets. "My performance as a doting husband obviously left a lot to be desired. Which is why my wives left." He'd discovered the hard way there was a big difference between the fantasy of family life and the reality.

Jordan...and Amelia...deserved better than what he could offer.

"You weren't in Erie then. But now you're home. It's not like you're going to be on your own. You know we'll all help.

I'll swing by to check on her at least once a week. Elke will help out. Hayden and Kara are both on summer vacation. You'll have so much help, you won't know what to do with it."

He blew out a long breath. Time to man up. After all, they *were* his kids. One look into Jordan's eyes told that truth. She was a Hawkins. "You leave me no choice."

"That's the spirit." Bethany looped her arm through his, heading for the door to Amelia's room. "But try to muster some enthusiasm, huh? Fake it if you have to. Don't make her feel worse than she already does.

"It's settled," Bethany announced as she gripped the rails of the hospital bed. "You and Jordan will be staying with Finn."

Amelia opened her eyes warily.

Bethany elbowed him.

"Right. I won't take no for an answer."

Amelia arched an eyebrow at them. "Jordan needs regular tests, treatments. Her hematologist—"

"We have hematologists in Erie," Bethany began. "In fact, we have—"

"If you tell me that another of the Hawkins tribe is a hematologist..."

"No hematologist in the family. But our brother Greg is an art therapist and he—"

"Oh, that will be helpful." Amelia closed her eyes again. "Maybe he can let me finger-paint as I slowly lose what's left of my sanity." The fetal monitor sped up as Amelia's heart rate increased. "Maybe I can sell the paintings instead of making money as a chiropractor. Yeah, that might work. Forget all that education. I can lie on my back, and someone can hold the paper over my head, and I can pretend I'm Michelangelo. That sounds like a plan."

"Amelia," Bethany snapped. "Take a deep breath and look at me."

She slowly opened her eyes.

"Thank you. Our brother Greg works with seriously ill kids. He's got close ties to the Children's Cancer Center here in town. They treat all the bone marrow failure diseases, including aplastic anemia, there. We have connections. We can make arrangements for Jordan right away, get her records sent down immediately, no problem at all."

Finn forced a grin. "No problem at all," he echoed.

Caring for a seriously ill teenager and a bedridden pregnant woman, both of whom he barely knew. Running a new restaurant, carving out a niche for himself in the local dining scene.

An unborn son, who'd been stitched into his mother's womb, and saddled with the enormous responsibility of saving his big sister's life. Problems?

Nah.

With his family dispersed to the parking garage and Elke getting a ride home from Kara, Finn crossed the walkway with Bethany, back to the office building. The excruciatingly long day had given way to evening. Streetlights flickered through the Plexiglas windows that lined the pedestrian bridge.

Inside the elevator, his sister leaned against the wall.

They exited on the ground floor. Finn escorted her to her car.

Bethany popped the automatic locks open. "Finn? One more thing we need to cover. It seems to me there's some chemistry between you and Amelia."

She had no idea about the intense chemistry they'd explored in his kitchen so many months ago. Still, physical attraction didn't amount to a hill of beans. Amelia didn't like him all that much. She'd made that clear. She certainly wasn't going to gush gratitude over his coming to the rescue.

"Trust me, Bethany, that woman would be halfway back to Maine already, without so much as a glance in the rearview window, if not for this complication. I don't think you have to worry."

She looked skeptical. "If you say so. Let me give you some advice as her doctor. Not only can't she have sex, which should be obvious—though I've learned from years in this business that nothing is as obvious as I think it is—but she's not to have an orgasm, either. By any means. In fact, I don't want that uterus to twitch at even the *thought* of an orgasm. I don't want her watching reruns of *Magnum P.I.* if Tom Selleck in his prime gets her hot and bothered. Got it?"

"Got it." He scowled down at his feet. No sex he'd guessed. Orgasm by other means he hadn't really contemplated, even though that was the only kind of sex they'd ever had. "Any other aspects about my sex life, or current lack thereof, you'd like to lecture me on before I head home?"

"You want the prevent-pregnancy-and-STDs-always-use-a-condom lecture for old times' sake?"

"No. I memorized that one years ago. Thanks."

"And yet you found a way around it to get a woman preg-

81

nant, anyway."

"Night, Bethany. Thanks again. I owe you one."

"You owe me more than one already, Beginagain, and you'll owe me even more before this is over." She gave him a quick hug, then slid into her car. "Chocolate mocha cheesecake is always appreciated."

"I'll see what I can do."

Back at the restaurant, he found Hayden and Jordan perched on the tall stools at the end of the serving counter of the work island. The video camera sat in front of them. Jordan, toying with the contents of her bowl, set down her spoon when he entered. "How's my mom? And the baby? Why hasn't she called me?"

"Both your mom and the baby are fine. She hasn't called you because she was really groggy from the medication they gave her for the operation. She said to tell you she'll call in the morning. And she said you're still grounded for life."

That coaxed a small smile from Jordan. "Now I know she's okay."

Finn peered into her bowl, finding a noxious-appearing concoction. Only a left-behind milky substance clung to the walls of Hayden's bowl. "What's this?"

"You're the chef," Hayden said. "You tell us."

"All right." He grabbed a tasting spoon from the plastic container on the work space. "The usual deal?" Stump the Chef was one of Hayden's favorite games. One he most often lost. "Yep."

Scooping up a hearty sample that included several lumps, Finn popped it into his mouth, rolled it across his tongue. After he swallowed, he began, "Vanilla ice cream, chocolate—"

"What kind of chocolate?" Hayden challenged.

"Mmmm...semisweet."

"Right. What else?"

"Whipped cream, triple chocolate brownies, cheesecake, and..." He rubbed his tongue across the roof of his mouth, searching for the final flavor, something that made sense only to Hayden. "Nutmeg?"

"I thought I'd get you with that one. Damn it." Hayden glanced at Jordan. "Excuse my French."

She gave his brother a broad grin and a look of absolute adoration that shot a dart of jealousy through Finn. Obviously Hayden had put the day to good use, bonding with *his* kid.

Jeez, he was starting to sound like Amelia. *My* daughter, *my* kid.

"S'okay," Jordan said.

"I get a free shot," Finn reminded his brother. "Assume the position."

"Free shot?" Jordan asked.

"It's the only way he ever gets one." Hayden slid from the stool, turning sidewise. "Go on."

Finn extended his middle knuckle, made a tight fist, then punched his brother, a former Marine, in the upper arm as hard as he could.

Hayden barely moved.

"Now. Tell me that you fed Jordan something besides a crazy dessert. As a Phys Ed teacher, I expect you to know better about nutrition."

"It's summer vacation. And I'm the uncle. I get to do the fun things. I don't have to make her eat her vegetables. That's your job."

Finn punched Hayden's arm again.

"Hey!" This time his brother rubbed the spot. "That wasn't fair."

"Good nutrition isn't optional."

"Next time I'll add some chia seeds. Oat bran. Maybe some broccoli."

Jordan stuck a finger in her mouth, gagging.

"There you go," Hayden said. "The kid has spoken."

Jordan then covered her mouth with her hand as she yawned widely.

"You need to get upstairs, brush your teeth so they don't rot out of your head after that so-called snack, and get ready for bed."

The left corner of Hayden's mouth curled. He gave Finn a covert thumbs-up combined with a quick head jerk. Once Jordan had started up the stairs, Hayden said, "Listen to you. Twenty-four hours into it and you sort of sounded like a dad just then."

Huh. Maybe this dad thing wasn't as hard as Finn thought.

CHAPTER SIX

THE LIGHT FROM JORDAN'S cell phone cast a blue glow into the room. Nearly midnight, and she'd tossed and turned. Being in this room last night, with its pansy wallpaper and the lavender bedspread, had been an adventure. A stolen moment she'd never expected to repeat.

Being here tonight, with Mom in the hospital, wasn't nearly as much fun.

This wasn't in either of their plans.

Her fingers danced over the keys, texting Shelby. She'd kept her friend updated about the crisis throughout the day, but Shelby had been busy getting ready to head to her dad's, so they hadn't really been able to chat. U awake?

It took a minute or two. Then the phone vibrated, and Shelby's response came in. Am now. Whazzup?

Can't sleep. It's 2 weird.

Sigh. Ok. Y weird?

Idk.

Yes u do. Ur worried about ur mom.

Duh.

And about baby?

Double duh.

What happens 2 u if something happens 2 baby?

Jordan tossed the phone to the floor on top of her jeans.

She grabbed the extra pillow and pulled it to her chest, curling around it. Leave it to Shelby to ask the question Jordan had avoided all day long.

Or tried to avoid, anyway.

It kept popping up, nagging her like Mom did when her room was a mess.

She forced her mind elsewhere. "Alan, Bethany, Cathy..." Uncle Hayden had told her the story of the twelve Hawkins siblings. How the first three had accidentally been named with A, B, C names. And how when baby number four was on the way, their parents had realized it, and decided to continue. "...Derek, Elke, Finn, Greg, Hayden, Ian, Judy, and Kara and Kyle, the twin babies of the family." Alphabetizing sure made memorizing them easier.

Jordan couldn't imagine what it must have been like to grow up with that many brothers and sisters. Always having someone to play with. Someone to share your secrets with. When she'd started kindergarten, she'd begged her mom for a brother or a sister.

But Mom always said no, that their family of two was perfect. That two was a lovely number. That she'd always planned on one child, because with a career, she wanted to give Jordan as much of her attention as possible, not spread it too thin.

Jordan's cell phone vibrated, muted by the clothes.

The need for a bone marrow donor when, against the odds, they hadn't been able to find one in the registry, had changed Mom's mind about a baby in a hurry.

And when Mom had a plan, she made it happen. Even when she hadn't gotten pregnant after the first two attempts at in vitro, Mom had tried to hide her emotions, assuring Jordan that "the third time's the charm."

And it had been.

Jordan had never imagined the possibility of outliving her baby sibling. Of the baby not even...

A gaping, hollow pit opened in her stomach.

She began to shake as her cell phone vibrated again.

Jolted from sleep by the shrill ring tone, one he'd chosen specifically to cut through the clatter and chaos of the kitchen, Finn grabbed for his phone, yanking it away from the charger on the night table.

His heart pounded against his rib cage, his first thought going to Amelia and Chip. "Hello?"

"Is this Jordan's dad?" asked an unfamiliar young girl's voice.

"Huh?"

"Finn Hawkins, right? Jordan's dad?"

He rubbed his eyes. "Uh, yeah. Who's this? And why are you calling me—" he blinked a few times to bring the blurry red numbers of his alarm clock into focus "—at 12:24 a.m.?"

"My name's Shelby. I'm Jordan's best friend. She sent me your phone number so I could keep it for her in case she forgot."

"And you're calling me because?"

"Oh. Because I was texting with JoJo and I think maybe she's upset. She won't answer me. Not by text, and not when I tried to call her."

"If you girls had a fight, I'm sure you can make up tomorrow. Jordan's probably sleeping. Like you should be." Like he should be. The delivery truck came early.

"No, it wasn't a fight. She's upset. Look, you have to go check on her! She doesn't ignore me."

"Okay, okay. I'll go check on her. Don't call back tonight, all right? I'll have Jordan call you tomorrow."

"All right. Thanks. Oh, and by the way...you sound as cute as you look."

The connection broke, leaving Finn staring at his lit phone. What the hell?

He shook his head as he clambered out of bed. He tossed on a pair of sweatpants and a T-shirt. His room was the largest, occupying the entire back of the house, over the kitchen. At one time, it had been the bridal suite of the bed-and-breakfast.

A few coats of paint and new furniture had transformed it into an appropriately masculine space.

The wooden floorboards in the hall creaked beneath his bare feet. Fortunately, he didn't have far to go. He'd put Jordan in the next room.

He leaned his ear to the inch-wide space where the door was cracked open. A long stretch of silence almost convinced him she was asleep, despite her friend's intuition, but then he heard a soft whimper.

He rapped lightly on the wood. "Jordan? Can I come in?"

No response. "Jordan, I'm coming in."

He pushed the door wide. Inside, the night-light from the attached bathroom provided enough illumination for him to maneuver around a pile of clothes on the floor.

It also showed the pajama-clad girl, half in, half out of the covers. Knees drawn up to her chest, she was curled into a ball, her back toward him.

"Hey? Are you okay?" Stupid question. Obviously she wasn't okay. Maybe he should call Alan or Derek. They had kids. Maybe even Greg. He would officially be a stepfather when Shannon married him in a few weeks.

Maybe Finn should call his mother.

When Jordan didn't respond, he laid a hand on her shoulder. She was trembling.

Alarmed, he shifted his palm to her cheek, then to her forehead. The fact that she didn't feel warm relieved him for all of two seconds. "Jordan?"

He eased himself onto the bed. Hesitated. Got back to his feet. Didn't seem like a great plan with a distraught adolescent girl he'd known for only a day. Even if he was technically her father.

He knelt on the braided rug alongside the bed and draped his arm over her shoulder, drawing her stiff, unyielding body into an awkward embrace. "What's wrong, kiddo? Talk to me."

She shook harder. "I—I c-can't stop it. C-can't stop thinking about it. Stupid brain. Shut up." She thumped her fist against her forehead.

He caught her hand. "Shhh. Don't do that. What can't you stop thinking about?"

"If—if the baby doesn't make it." She hiccupped. "Then I—I won't make it."

Pain radiated through his chest, as if a searing hot knife had slid between his ribs. He rocked her in his arms.

"It's not the plan. Not the plan! *My* plan...Mom didn't know..." The girl gulped. "My plan was that even if the transplant didn't work, then Mom wouldn't be alone. She'd still have a family." Jordan sniffled. "She'd still have the new baby."

"Chip," Finn murmured, unsure how to deal with the teen's fears. Where the hell was Greg when he needed him? He was the expert when it came to dealing with stuff like this. "Huh?"

"Chip. The new baby is a boy."

"A boy? I'm getting a brother?"

"Yep. Is that okay?"

"I suppose. I was hoping for a girl, but..." Her shoulder twitched beneath his arm. "Why is his name Chip?"

"Nickname. Because apparently your mom craves potato chip and marshmallow fluff sandwiches."

A chuckle made her seem to shake more. "Yeah. I tried one. Gross."

"Sounds gross. Like something Hayden might try to put together."

The lumps of the rug burned his knees. Finn shifted. The silence stretched between them, and Jordan's trembling intensified. He cleared his throat and prayed for divine intervention. Jordan to suddenly fall asleep. The house to catch on fire. Anything to rescue him from this situation. Barring that, he'd settle for something inspired to say.

"Let me tell you what I think about planning. Planning is good. Within reason. Like, I plan my menus a week in advance. I plan for special parties months in advance. But I'm always flexible. Open to changes. Because, say, the market might have some really great produce that I hadn't expected. Your mom's a big planner, isn't she?"

Jordan's body began to relax beneath his arm. "Yeah. She started planning for high school in elementary school, because she already knew she wanted to go to college. In college she planned for chiropractic school, planned her life. Mom says you should always have a plan."

"And I'll tell you something my nanna used to say. 'We plan, God laughs.'"

"What's that mean?"

"It means God's in control, not us. His plans are often different than ours would be. People are nearsighted. We can only see a small part of the picture. For example—" he stroked her silky dark hair "—if you hadn't gotten sick, you and I would never have met. I'm not glad you're sick, not at all. I'd change it in an instant if I could. But I'm glad that it brought you here. To me."

"Me, too." She squeezed his forearm.

Her gesture warmed him. "And because of this crisis with Chip, we're going to get to spend even more time together."

"We are?" She wiggled, then flipped over to face him, still clutching the pillow.

"Oh, crap. Your mother's going to kill me. I wasn't supposed to tell you that. She wanted to talk to you about it herself."

"How long?"

Finn pressed his lips together.

"I'll pretend I don't know when Mom tells me."

"The rest of her pregnancy. Three months."

"Three months? Mom's going to be in the hospital for three months?" Jordan sat up, forcing him to lean back. "I'm not going to get to see her that long?"

Finn rose slowly, knees protesting. "No, no. She's not going to be in the hospital."

"Where will she be?"

"Here. You and your mom will be staying here. She has to stay in bed all the time, except I think Bethany said she's allowed up to go to the bathroom. And that's basically it."

"We're staying here? With you? For three months?"

"Yes." In the soft light, he could see the play of emotions across her face. "Is that a bad thing?"

"Well...Shelby will be gone all summer, anyway. School is over, and since I have my computer, I could do cyberschool from here if I had to. I'm going to do cyberschool when I have my transplant." She glanced at Finn, then down at the bedspread. "Hmmm. No." She looked back up at him. "This is a good thing."

"I'm glad you think so. Now, we both need to get some sleep." He pulled back the covers. "Get in here."

After fixing the pillows, she popped between the sheets. He covered her, then tucked the bedspread tightly around her form.

Two failed marriages, both over before the first anniversary, had convinced him he wasn't family material. Didn't have the stuff to be a husband, let alone a father. But apparently he did have some dad instincts. There was something satisfying about it. No wonder his father had always been there at bedtime, no matter what pressing cases he was working on.

"Good night." As Finn moved to leave, Jordan grabbed his hand.

"Will you stay a little longer? Just until I fall asleep? In case my brain still won't shut up?"

Okay, so Parenting 101, tucking a kid in, he'd managed. He'd even distracted her for a bit. But the advanced stuff... How did you reassure a child with a legitimate fear of dying?

If he said the wrong thing, he could really mess her up.

Not to mention Amelia would have his head.

"If you want." This time he perched on the edge of the bed, still holding Jordan's hand.

"I memorized the list of all your brothers and sisters. Alan, Bethany, Cathy, Derek, Elke, Finn, Greg, Hayden, Ian, Judy, Kara & Kyle."

"Impressive."

"Tell me something about one of them."

"Okay." He thought about it for a few moments. "Let me tell you something I learned from Ian."

She wrapped her other hand over his. "Uncle Hayden wouldn't talk about him. He got quiet, and wouldn't say anything about him except he died years ago."

"Hayden and Ian were really close. They were only ten months apart, and in the same grade at school. It's still hard for Hayden to talk about him."

"Oh. I didn't know."

Finn squeezed her fingers. "Of course you didn't. Don't worry about it. Anyway..."

"How did he die?"

"That's not important to the story." In fact, that was probably the last thing she needed to hear right now. Though she didn't have the same disease, she also faced increased risks of infection while waiting for her bone marrow transplant. "Ian didn't teach me anything about dying." Again, not completely true. Courage, grace and irreverent humor had been Ian's response to his cancer. "He taught me about living to the fullest. He did what he wanted to do, even though sometimes our parents got really ticked at him for it." Finn chuckled. "Sort of like someone I know, who took off on an adventure to meet her father, making her mother mad."

"Last night Kara said something to Hayden about Ian knocking a woman up. Was that one of those things?"

In the dim light of the room, Finn grinned. "Oh, yeah, that was one of those things. Our parents fumed for months, especially when Ian didn't get married. But it was almost as if he knew he had to cram a lot into nineteen years. He didn't know, of course. And that's the point. Nanna used to say, 'yesterday is history, tomorrow is a mystery, today is a gift.' Right now. That's all we really have. This moment. So you've got to enjoy it while it's here. Don't dwell too much on the past, or the future, okay?"

"Only now. This moment."

"Exactly. And for this moment, you're safe, you're snuggled into a comfortable bed and your mom and brother are both doing well. All's right in the world." Hopefully, Finn sounded convincing. He wasn't sure much of anything was right in his world.

Lying didn't seem like it should be part of the parenting toolbox. Although lying to comfort a scared child didn't seem all that horrible. After all, Santa Claus and the Tooth Fairy were part of the parenting arsenal, too.

Jordan removed one of her hands to stifle a yawn, then closed her eyes.

Finn released a slow sigh of relief. He waited long after her breathing had evened out before he disentangled his fingers from her now-limp ones.

The last thing he needed was to wake her up.

Entering Finn's home for the third time wasn't the charm. Far from it.

Especially since this trip had been taken in a medical transport van with Amelia tied to a stretcher. And she faced three months of exile.

In his house.

She'd willingly—eagerly—sacrificed many things, money, her body, her pride—even risked her career—to save Jordan's life.

But three months in Finn's house...this was going to be the hardest. Because she had to keep him from getting too close to any of them. Not just physically, though after the terrifying lecture on orgasms and cervical sutures from his sister, the doctor, Amelia wasn't as concerned about the potent chemistry they'd explored that day so long ago. Just having Jordan in the house with her put a damper on that.

The emotional ramifications scared her more.

Depending on someone made you weak. Being weak made you vulnerable. And Amelia Young didn't do vulnerable. Not anymore.

She'd learned as a child you couldn't trust anyone. Despite that, she'd trusted a man. One who'd seemed like a prince.

That hadn't worked out so well.

Fortunately, Finn seemed as reluctant about the situation as she was. As long as they both kept their distance, everything would be fine.

The stretcher bounced precariously on the sidewalk. She gripped the side bars as they carried her up the stairs to the porch. Someone had opened both sets of double doors in the foyer, and the crew halted inside.

Late luncheon customers in the dining room stared, and Amelia wanted to crawl into a hole.

"Mom, Mom!" Jordan barreled down the main staircase, prepared to throw herself at Amelia.

"Easy!" Finn, hot on her heels and wearing his chef's jacket, grabbed her by the shoulder, slowing her down. "Don't jostle her."

Amelia held her arms open, trying not to lift her head too much. "Flat on your back" had been pounded into her by the nurses over the past two days. Jordan eased into the embrace.

"I missed you so much."

"I missed you, too, honey."

"Let's get her settled, then you can visit, okay?" the burly female attendant said.

Finn cast a concerned glance over Amelia at his dining room. "Good idea." He ushered Jordan away from the stretcher, which started to move forward.

Amelia raised a hand. "You're not carrying me up those stairs on this thing. No way."

"It's perfectly safe." The male paramedic at her head patted her shoulder. "We do this stuff all the time."

"No."

"Well, you're not supposed to walk up them," Finn said. "Bethany's instructions were clear. You can get up to go to the bathroom. Period."

"Bathroom's on the second floor, right?" Amelia gripped the railings again.

Finn's brother Hayden—she'd learned to identify him from the cell phone pictures Jordan had sent—said in a low voice, "Easy enough, dumbass. Pick her up and carry her." He flipped off the "seat belts" strapped over her and peeled back the lightweight blanket they'd covered her with.

Though terrified of going up the stairs on the stretcher, Amelia didn't want Hayden hoisting her, either. Bulging biceps at the arms of his T-shirt assured her he was strong enough, but still... "Please, don't—"

Finn elbowed his brother out of the way. "I got her."

With a wide grin, Hayden offered Finn a sweeping bow. Jordan giggled.

Finn slid one arm under her knees, the other behind her shoulders. Before she could protest again, he'd scooped her against his chest and was striding toward the stairs.

She clasped her hands behind his neck. "This is so not necessary."

"It's me or the stretcher. Actually, now it's me. Decision made." He began to climb. "Thanks, guys," he called to the medical transport team, dismissing them.

Being in his arms definitely felt more secure. His breath, warm against the side of her face, carried the scent of strong coffee. Beneath that lingered a more exotic mixture of soap and male sweat and something uniquely Finn.

Her stomach tightened in response.

And Dr. Hawkins's warnings about arousal came flooding back. Amelia began to hum softly.

Finn raised his eyebrows at her as he topped the stairs.

"The theme song from *Gilligan's Island?*"

"Yep."

"May I ask why?"

To distract from his presence didn't seem like a wise thing to confess, especially with Jordan following right behind them. There was nothing even remotely sexy about Gilligan. "'Cause my three-hour tour has turned into a God-only-knows-when-this-will-end stranding?"

"Ah. Okay."

He carried her partway down the hall, hesitated briefly near a door, then continued the length of the house.

"Where we going?" Jordan asked from behind them. "I thought—"

"I changed my mind. I think your mom will be more comfortable down here."

"This is my room," Jordan announced as they passed the final door on the left. To the right, the back staircase loomed.

Going straight, Finn entered a spacious room at the end of the hall. Inside the door to one side, a queen-size bed with a dark brown comforter hugged the tan wall. On the opposite side was a matching chest of drawers.

Beyond the bed, a dark raspberry sofa with an attached chaise longue sat in a corner created by walls Amelia assumed had something to do with closets and a bath. Opposite the sofa, a big-screen television dominated the wall, framed by a black media center with storage towers. Heavy, floor-length brown drapes had been pulled back from sliding glass doors to reveal a deck overlooking the lake.

A sneaking suspicion began to nag at her.

As they crossed to the bed, Finn jerked an elbow in the direction of a door, confirming her theory with, "Bathroom's in there."

The apron on the hook near the bathroom door clinched it. "This is your room, isn't it?"

"Not anymore." He maneuvered around the foot of the bed, carrying her to the far side.

"You said you had empty rooms!"

"I do. And I'll move into one of them." He shrugged. "It's not a big deal. You're going to be stuck here 24/7, so..."

"Isn't it pretty?" Jordan rested her forehead against the glass, staring out at the tranquil blue water. White clouds hung over it like giant cotton balls.

"Yes, Jordan, it is."

Finn eased Amelia down onto the bed, cutting off her view. She quickly assumed "the position," flat on her back to remove the pressure from her cervix. God only knew how much they'd put on it getting her up here.

Finn hovered at the foot of the bed.

"Thank you," she told him. "It wasn't necessary for you to give up your room, but I appreciate it." She didn't know what to make of it, though. And that made her apprehensive. The man who'd protested her staying at his house worked better for her. Toad behavior actually made her more comfortable.

Better the toad you knew than a toad hiding in a prince costume.

His uncertainty gave way to that slow, sexy grin, the one that made her want to hum *Gilligan's Island* theme music again.

She wished he'd show his warts.

His eyes twinkled, as though he suspected what was going

on in her mind. "You're welcome. Listen, I have to get back to the kitchen. Bethany said she'd stop by tonight to check on you. If you need anything, send Jordan down, or Hayden. He lives here, too, and if he's home, he'll also be at your service. Or call my cell phone."

Finn headed for the door. The black pants he wore beneath the white chef's jacket didn't do him justice. Not like the butt-hugging jeans he'd worn yesterday morning to visit her in the hospital.

Given all the problems she faced, she had no business ogling his ass.

But...if she dwelled too long on the other stuff, she'd snap.

He paused in the doorway. "You hungry now?"

She shook her head. *With Gilligan, the Skipper, too...*

It was going to be a long three months.

With lunch service over, and dinner service yet to begin, Finn checked his stocks. The walk-in fridge. The soup of the day. The amount of prepped food. And tried to ignore that Amelia was now ensconced in the room over his head.

Which became near impossible when the dragging noises started. Big items sliding along the floor. Ceiling.

What the hell was going on up there?

Leaving the kitchen under the watchful—mostly—eye of his sous-chef, Finn washed his hands and climbed the back staircase.

"What's going on?" he asked from the doorway to his bedroom.

Hayden and Kara, each on one end of his bed, paused in

the process of shoving it closer to the sliding glass doors. Hayden shrugged, giving Finn his best "just doin' my job, boss" look. The sofa now stood where his bed had been. Amelia lay flat on the chaise portion of it.

"Get those papers filled out," she said into her cell phone, "then scan and e-mail them to me. I should have my computer set up shortly. I want to make sure the staff is taken care of with unemployment. I'll call you back later." She ended the call and glanced over at him.

"I'm sorry," she said. "I probably should have asked you before moving the furniture. I just thought it would be a lot nicer to have the bed over by the doors, so I can see the lake. And the television. Makes more sense this way, doesn't it?"

She'd been there less than two hours, and already she was completely rearranging his life. Changing things.

It was one thing for him to change them—like offering her his room. Something else for her to do it.

"Of course it's better," Kara chirped. "At least this way you can see the outside world."

"Why aren't you making sure the dining room is ready for dinner?" Finn asked his sister.

"Because I'm *helping*. Besides, I already went over it. It's ready. On three..." Kara counted, and she and Hayden finished positioning the bed.

"Perfect," Amelia announced. "Thank you." She got up from the chaise.

"What are you doing?" Finn demanded.

She paused, propping a fist on her hip. "Getting in bed, what does it look like? I'm allowed to be up for a few minutes at a time."

Kara pulled back the covers on the freshly made bed. The sheets had been changed, too.

He hadn't thought about that touch when he'd impulsively plonked her in his bedroom.

Try to be nice, and what did it get you?

Guilt. For not thinking of all the right details.

"Looks like you've got everything under control here," he said. "I'm going back to my kitchen."

At least there he knew what he was doing.

CHAPTER SEVEN

AFTER A VERY SUCCESSFUL Friday night a week and a half later, Finn locked up. The only light still on, over the island, reflected in the gleaming surfaces. Sanitizer lingered in the air. A sparkling kitchen on the heels of a very busy night deeply gratified him.

He kicked off his clogs at the base of the stairs, ready for the next morning. He'd already tossed his jacket in the dirty linens basket. On the second floor, he paused outside his bedroom. Former bedroom.

Though the door was ajar, he knocked softly. "Amelia?"

He heard a faint sigh in the dim room. "I'm sorry. Amelia's not available to take your call right now. She's run off to a tropical paradise with Sven, the blond massage therapist. If you'll leave a message, she'll ignore it."

Finn chuckled. "Okay, then I won't bother. I stopped by to see if she needed anything before I hit the sack. Something to eat? Drink?"

She snorted. "If I drink now, I'll have to pee before morning. Your sister already lectured me on getting up too many times. Threatened to bedpan me. Just what I need, to lose the remaining shred of my dignity. So thanks, but no thanks."

A somber note of desperation, with a side order of hysteria, ran beneath the words. He stepped in as his eyes adjusted to the light. Or lack thereof.

The sliding glass door curtains were open. Outside, stars flickered over the lake.

He crossed the room toward the bed. She lay on the far side, closest to the deck. After moving her laptop, cell phone, the TV remote, a book and a magazine, Finn eased himself on top of the comforter, lying on his side, facing her. He dug his elbow into the mattress, leaned his ear in his palm. "So, how was your day?"

"Oh, my day was fabulous. I had luncheon with the girls at the club. Then we went to the spa. Sven, unable to resist, seduced me in the massage room. To top it off, I took a private jet to New York for dinner. I only got back a few minutes ago, and I'm exhausted."

"Where'd you eat in the city? *What* did you eat?"

She finally turned her head in his direction. "That's all you want to know about? What I ate?"

He grinned. "I *am* a chef. I'm wondering how I measure up to the competition."

"But you don't want to know how you measure up to Sven? I thought manhood came first, then occupation. I'm crushed that you're not jealous. I mean, here I am, living in your house, carrying your baby, sleeping in your bed..."

The temperature in the room spiked.

She flipped her head to look out the doors again, cursing under her breath.

He struggled to wrestle his desire into submission. *Off-limits.*

"Let's try that again," she murmured. "My day was uneventful, as usual. How was yours?"

Bethany's nagging voice rang in his head. If anyone could

put a damper on his sexual urges, it was Dr. STD Lecture. "Busy. We did seventy-two covers tonight."

"Covers?"

"Meals. Dinners?"

"Oh. That's good. It sounded sort of busy down there."

"You can hear it?"

She lifted one shoulder. "Mostly it's low-level background noise. Although...every once in a while, I can hear you yelling at someone."

His cheeks flushed. "Gotta keep them on their toes somehow."

"I kind of like it. Makes me feel less isolated."

He grinned. "Okay. I'll make a note to yell more often, then. My staff might get annoyed, but hey, I'd like to make my houseguest comfortable."

"I don't think comfort is in my immediate future." She shifted beneath the blanket. "The human body was not designed for this."

"Having a baby?"

"Lying on your back twenty-three hours a day. I move as much as I can, but this..." She blew out a long breath. "This has gotten old already."

"I'm sorry."

"Not your fault, right?"

"Right." Raging hormone crisis—his, not hers—averted. On to the serious things they needed to cover. Like the visit from his lawyer sister. "Cathy gave me those medical forms for Jordan you signed today. The ones that grant me permission to approve treatment for her so I can take her to the hematologist Monday." He'd tried to get Elke to do it. Or anybody else. But because Fresh was closed on Mondays, they'd all declined, leaving it to him. "They've got all her records now. And I have her insurance card."

Amelia pressed her lips tightly together. "As long as you remember it's temporary. It's *all* temporary."

"So you keep reminding me. I get it, Amelia. You're not happy about needing my help. Can't say that I blame you. But really, neither of us had many options, did we?"

She didn't respond.

"Should I have said no to more sperm to save Jordan? Should I have let you spend the rest of your pregnancy in the hospital? Or some nursing facility? Let social services take custody of Jordan until you could get a friend from Maine to come fetch her? What kind of guy would I be if I'd done any of those things?"

"A typical one?"

The note of uncertainty in her normally confident tone pulled at him. "Maybe. Or maybe you just have crappy taste in men." He skimmed his fingers along her arm. "Somebody's obviously burned you. But it wasn't me. And I'll be damned if I'm going to pay for his mistakes. I'm not perfect." He barked a wry laugh. "Ask my ex-wives. They'll be happy to provide a list of my sins and shortcomings. But I refuse to be classified as evil scum just because I have a penis."

"Ex-wives?" She emphasized the *s*. "How many?"

"Two."

"Really? What happened?"

He'd failed, was what happened. Hadn't lived up to their expectations. "My first wife didn't appreciate the long days—and nights—I spent at the restaurants. She didn't realize that being married to a chef is like being married to a doctor. Or a lawyer. She thought it was going to be one big dinner party."

"And the second? Did she feel neglected by your work, too?"

He shook his head. "I made it clear before the wedding that I worked long hours and wouldn't likely be home to share very many dinners with her."

"So what happened?"

"Marianna decided, despite what we'd agreed on before getting married, that she wanted a baby. Right away. And she didn't listen when I told her I wasn't ready. I found out she'd stopped taking her birth control pills without telling me. A big fight and a load of tears later, she decided she wanted a baby more than she wanted to wait for me to be ready to be a dad." That had stung. Far more than he'd ever admitted to anyone.

"And now?"

"Now what?"

"Are you ready to be a dad now?"

"Relax, Amelia. No. I'm not. Jordan is safe. I'm not going to ask for joint custody or anything." Which had made the last week-and-a-half awkward. Every time Jordan looked at him with those hopeful eyes, he'd wanted to run the other way. Yeah, he made great father material.

"Did your ex-wife get her baby? Did she know about your sperm donation?"

No one had. Not even his brothers. Had Marianna known he had biological kids out in the world somewhere, but wasn't willing to give her any, she'd have waffled between seriously pissed and crushed.

"You know..." He leaned toward Amelia, anxious to change

the mood. "You're awfully interested in my ex-wives for someone who doesn't even like me."

"I never said I didn't like you."

"So you do?"

"I didn't say that, either." The corners of her mouth twitched.

That was more like it. "Admit it." He turned one of his slow, sexy grins loose. "You like me."

"You're...growing on me."

"Ha. See? I knew it."

"Like a fungus." She laughed, the rich sound warming him.

He preferred her company a lot more when she was smiling, or laughing. Or... Okay, not going back *there* again. "Nice. You've been hanging out with Hayden too much."

Hayden had willingly pitched in with both Amelia and Jordan, leaving Finn better able to run Fresh.

Of course, the whole family was helping out, just as Bethany had promised. Elke came to do nursing stuff, including assisting Amelia with her personal care. Bethany made house calls. Greg had been a lifeline for Finn's questions, and had added Jordan to his art therapy group, despite being hip-deep in wedding preparations. Their mother had been to visit several times, bringing reading material to keep Amelia occupied.

Finn's questions about Amelia's family, whether she wanted her own mother to come and help, evoked the frosty assertion that her relationship with her mother worked best long distance only and generally was limited to phone calls several times a year when her mother needed money. And that Finn had now spent more time with Jordan in a week and a half than her grandmother had ever spent with her.

The reason for her stubborn independence became clear in that moment.

"So...seriously. How's it going? The bed rest thing, I mean."

"You want the truth?"

"Yeah. Always."

"This is the hardest thing I've done in my life, Finn. Everyone's been really helpful, even Jordan, but..." Amelia sighed. "Today she made me create a Facebook page. I now have a *Facebook page*, Finn."

He tried not to laugh.

"I have five friends already, and they can read my wall when I post about...oh, I don't know...the clouds floating by the window, or spilling water on myself for the umpteenth time.

"I want my life back. I want to wear real clothes. Or at least real maternity clothes. Nightshirts and muumuus and other non-binding-in-the-middle sacks do not an acceptable wardrobe make. I want to get back to work!"

"I'm sorry." Unable to resist, he brushed the back of his finger over her cheek. "It's got to be driving you crazy. But you're doing really important work *here*. You're growing a baby, Amelia. A human being. Think how extraordinary that is. And if that's not enough, you're saving Jordan's life right now, too. I think that's a pretty damn big, important job. I'm in awe of you."

She cleared her throat, turning her head away from him. He withdrew his hand. She bit down on her lip.

"I'm serious. You're an amazing woman."

She looked at him again, scrunching her eyebrows. "Yeah?"

"Yeah." He pressed his lips to her forehead, smoothing the tension lines. Moving slightly lower, he planted a kiss on the tip of her nose. Then he hovered just over her mouth, feeling the warmth of her breath.

With every bit of tenderness he could muster, he feathered his mouth over hers. An amuse-bouche.

But she wasn't nouvelle cuisine. No. As he indulged himself in one more kiss, he knew with a certainty.

Amelia was home-cooking.

Comfort food. Blue jeans and Sunday dinner.

Things he'd never really expected to find outside of his parents' house.

But his mouth on hers felt more than a little comfortable. Not daring to take it any deeper, he pulled away. When her eyes fluttered open, there was bemusement in them.

He gave her a quick grin, then slid lower on the bed. "Good night, Chip," he said to her belly. "Let your mother get some sleep, okay?" The wooden floor was cool beneath Finn's feet as he padded from the room.

He paused in the doorway. "You're growing on me, Amelia Young. And not like a fungus."

And that scared the hell out of him. Falling for her wouldn't just bring him the usual complications of a woman in his life.

She came with a lot more baggage.

One-point-five children, to be exact. Children who would expect things from him.

Playing at being a temporary daddy was one thing. Close

enough to fantasy, not the ugly glare of reality.

Considering keeping them in his life...not possible. For either of them.

Damn it, he needed to keep more distance from her. Before somebody got hurt.

Amelia's brain was stuck on one thing: last night, he'd kissed her.

Not like that first time. Not all-consuming. Not a prelude to seduction. Or at least, prelude to foreplay. Tender. Sweet.

And she'd thought of little else since.

Which was beyond stupid. Amelia Young didn't moon over a man.

Scowling, she set her fingers back to the keyboard of the laptop she had positioned on the tilted desk made specifically for use on a bed. She'd found it on the Internet and it definitely made typing a lot easier.

Her article on bed rest and back pain, documenting the stretches and other techniques she'd come up with to help minimize the pain and impact of lying on her back all the time, just wasn't working. She opened a new document.

"Mom, check this out!" Jordan, carrying her own laptop, rushed through the bedroom door, Hayden one step behind her.

Her daughter jumped onto the bed, turning the computer to face Amelia. "Look what Uncle Hayden did."

All the Hawkins siblings had been granted aunt and uncle status. Finn's parents had become Grandma Lydia and Papa Michael. But to Amelia's relief, Jordan hadn't bestowed any form of "dad" on Finn.

Like she knew his heart wasn't in it.

Amelia's daughter had good instincts.

On the screen, Finn diced vegetables at the workstation in the kitchen. The view came from higher up, and Amelia had an excellent view of the stoves and island—his two main work areas. Sound accompanied the video images, and she could now clearly hear him calling orders to his staff as they prepared for Saturday's lunch customers.

"Okay. Why am I watching the kitchen?"

Hayden grinned. "Finn mentioned that you feel isolated up here. I thought giving you a window to the kitchen might help."

"I see. And is your brother aware of this?"

The grin widened. "Sort of. He gave me permission to do it. He just doesn't know yet that I did. I imagine when he does his closing inspection tonight he'll find it. And then I plan to set up his laptop on the shelf there so that he can communicate back to you. But for now..."

"But for now, we're spying on him!" Jordan giggled, gazing at Hayden with adoration.

Oh, hell. Maybe Jordan's instincts weren't as honed yet as Amelia thought. Hayden oozed charm from every pore—making him the least savory of men, from Amelia's experience. The kind you really had to watch out for.

The toad-in-prince-clothing kind. The kind she'd once made the mistake of marrying, despite all the lessons about men she'd supposedly learned in her own childhood.

At least Finn didn't hide his toadiness.

"If you let me borrow your computer for a few minutes, I'll

get it set up so you can tap into the camera." Hayden held out his hand.

"Maybe you'll pick up some cooking tips, Mom."

"Oh, that's nice. Thanks for the vote of confidence." Amelia checked the clock. "Actually, our lunch should be here soon. Go wash up."

"Okay." Jordan headed for the en suite bathroom.

Amelia closed her documents and unplugged the laptop from the power cord, passing it to Hayden. "Thanks."

He sat on the couch, tapping at the keyboard. By the time Jordan came back to the bed and snuggled up alongside her, he had it done. "You want me to go downstairs and bring your lunch up?"

Amelia pursed her lips, struggling to control a grin of her own. "Not yet."

At that moment, Finn barked, "Jon, see who the hell is knocking on the back door."

The lanky teenager scurried across the camera's field. A minute later he reappeared, hesitantly approaching Finn with a brown bag in his hand.

"What, Jon?" Finn snapped.

"Uh, Chef. This was delivered for Amelia." The kid set the bag on the edge of the island work space and quickly backed away. "I, uh, I'm going to go make sure we've got everything ready in the dining room."

Hayden leaned over the bed for a better look.

Finn set down his knife and lifted the bottom of the white paper stapled to the bag. Then he cursed a blue streak, whipping out his cell phone.

Amelia reached for her phone before it even rang. "Hello?"

"What the hell is this? You ordered Chinese food delivered to *my* restaurant?"

Hayden snorted.

"I have all sorts of wonderful food down here, ready for you at a moment's notice. I can even cook Chinese, if that's what you want. Especially Beef and Broccoli. All you had to do was ask. And you order crap brought into my place."

"Did you cash my room and board checks yet?" She'd given him the first check the day they'd brought her from the hospital. She'd given him another yesterday.

He paced the space between the stoves and the island. "Not yet. Haven't had a chance."

"Don't give me that. You send someone to the bank every damn workday. Until you're willing to let me pay my own way, then we're not eating your food. I can't do anything about living under your roof, but I can manage to get other food."

"You don't know the quality of the ingredients in this." He slapped at the bag. "You don't know if they dumped a load of MSG in here."

"No MSG."

"And you believed them? But how can you be *sure?*"

"I'm sending Jordan downstairs for the food. I'd appreciate some utensils." She nudged Jordan until the girl slipped off the bed and hesitantly left the room.

"The hell you are." Finn snapped his phone shut and crammed it into his pocket. Then he grabbed the bag and headed out of sight.

"What's he up to?" Amelia asked.

Downstairs, a door slammed.

Hayden rounded the foot of the bed. He opened the sliding glass doors and went onto the deck, letting in the warm late-June air. He returned, shaking his head. "Your Chinese delivery just went into the Dumpster out back."

"Unfreakin' believable. That was mean." She'd be deducting the cost of the meal from her next room and board check.

Hayden latched the glass doors. "Do you have any idea how deeply you just wounded him?"

"He wouldn't take my money."

"Another blow to a man's ego. Look, Finn's uncertain with all this. He's doing what he can. And what he can do is cook. Feed you. And you just told him you prefer someone else's food. For him, that's like a lover telling him she'd prefer someone else in the sack. You just admitted you did it because he wouldn't take your money. Not because you wanted the food, but because you wanted to teach him a lesson, right? So before you call *him* mean..." Hayden jerked the bedroom door closed behind him, leaving her alone.

Amelia sank back into her pillow. The kitchen cam showed Finn barking new orders at his staff, scowling as he worked. Until Jordan appeared. Then he pasted on a smile for her, ushering her to a stool at the end of the island so she could watch while he prepared several plates.

Amelia had to grudgingly admit he *was* trying.

Which meant no more take-out orders. She reached for her cell to mollify him.

Finn slammed pans on the stove a lot harder than he should have. But every time he turned to face Jordan, he didn't let it show. It wasn't the kid's fault. *She* hadn't ordered food from the dive down the street.

He wiped his hands on his apron. "So, Jordan, what can I get you for lunch? I've got your mom's Beef and Broccoli just about ready, but can you think of something else she might like?"

"I'll have some of the five cheese pastina."

"You got it." The upscale version of mac-and-cheese had been a big hit, not just with Jordan, but with most of his customers.

Jordan propped her chin in her hand. "I don't know what Mom wants. Besides pumpkin pie."

"Pumpkin pie? It's not the right time of the year for pumpkin pie."

Jordan shrugged. "I heard her mention it when she was on the phone to Sia this morning."

Sia was Amelia's best friend, who also managed her office. Amelia spent a lot of time on the phone with her, going over work details. Finn had overheard several conversations where his stuck-in-bed mom-to be lamented her situation.

After several near disasters, they'd discovered that finger foods worked best for a bedridden person. In a normal household, that would mean a lot of chicken tenders, French fries, and carrot and celery sticks for veggies. But when you had a personal chef to cook for you...

Too bad she didn't appreciate his skills.

Hayden came from the back staircase, a large green duffel bag in his hand. He paused alongside Jordan. "You got things under control here? Keeping an eye on the chef to make sure he doesn't burn anything?"

Jordan nodded. "What's in the bag?"

"I'd tell you, but then I'd have to kill you."

"Uncle Hay-den! Come on."

He leaned over, spoke in a stage whisper. "Can you keep a secret?"

Jordan nodded.

"You won't blow my cover, right?"

"I promise."

"I'm a superhero. My gear is in here." He lifted the bag and drew back the zipper, exposing a flash of yellow spandex.

"Oh, puh-leeze. I heard all about Captain Chemo from Uncle Greg. That's not a secret."

Hayden clutched the bag to his chest, lower lip quivering. "Hopefully the kids at Cleveland Clinic, where the captain is due for an appearance this afternoon, will believe better than you do. Poor Captain Chemo. You've hurt his feelings."

"He'll get over it. Will you see any kids today who've had bone marrow transplants?"

Finn froze, pan in midair as he tossed the beef and broccoli.

Hayden lifted an eyebrow at him, but looked at Jordan as he answered. "The bone marrow transplant unit is harder to get into than Fort Knox. If any kids are almost ready to go home, we might see them. Why?"

Finn had read a bone marrow transplant handbook posted by the Portland hospital on their site. He hadn't been in the loop during Ian's illness, and wanted to understand just what Jordan would go through. Visitors were strictly limited in the early post-transplant days, and thorough precautions ensured the dangers of infection were kept in check as much as possible. The chemo before a BMT completely wiped out the immune system, and until the new bone marrow began to produce cells in great enough numbers, the recipient had no defense.

Jordan shrugged. "Just curious."

"You know what? I think one of Greg's kids who's had a bone marrow transplant will be at the wedding. You could talk to him about it then if you want."

Three weeks tomorrow, Finn's brother, Greg, would shackle himself to Shannon. Hopefully they'd have better luck with marriage than he had. Especially since he really liked Shannon. The ceremony itself would take place behind Fresh, on the bluff overlooking the lake. Shannon wasn't a church-wedding kind of girl.

Finn had offered to do the reception, but as with everything else, Shannon had her own ideas—ideas that left his mother and sisters shaking their heads. He was in the wedding party and she wanted him to have a good time, too.

Then there were her restrictions on clothes. Rented or secondhand only.

"There's going to be a boy there who's had a BMT?"

"I think so, yeah," Hayden said. "A lot of Greg's kids will be there."

Jordan had met some of them earlier that morning, when she'd had her first session with his cancer kids art therapy group.

"Am I invited?"

Hayden shot Finn a look that said *answer her.*

Finn waved the pan in his hand, shaking his head.

Hayden glared at him. Then he put his finger under Jordan's chin and lifted it. "What did I tell you the night we met about the one thing a Hawkins values above all else?"

"F-family."

"That's right." His brother's dark expression and pointed stare proved he was talking more to Finn than the kid. "So of course you're invited. You and your mom are *family*. Right, Finn?"

"Absolutely." His stomach tightened.

Ready or not, like it or not, they *were* family.

His family.

And he would do his best to live up to that responsibility.

CHAPTER EIGHT

"**ARE YOU SURE** you're up to this?" Finn glanced across his Explorer as he pulled into Wegmans' parking lot the next day. Dark smudges underlined Jordan's eyes. "You look tired."

She lifted one shoulder. "I told you, I'm fine. This is your grocery store? It's gigantic."

Finn let it drop. "For a chain grocery store, this place is amazing." He'd fed everyone Sunday breakfast, but wanted to fulfill Amelia's pumpkin pie craving. Plus he had an idea to break up the monotony of her day, but he needed Jordan and her video camera to do it.

Inside, he offered the cart to Jordan. Whenever he took one of his nieces to the store, she always wanted to push the basket. Jordan shook her head. "Mom says the handles on those things are like, one of the worst places for germs."

Finn steered it to the wall, pulled a sanitizing wipe from a dispenser, and thoroughly cleaned the handle. "Okay now?"

Jordan shrugged. "I guess." She leaned onto the basket as she maneuvered it through the store's foyer, dodging a mom pulling a shrieking toddler by the hand. The scents of coffee and fresh roasting chickens filled the air.

A bunch of pink roses caught his attention in the flower section. Amelia didn't strike him as the pink roses type. But if he was going to try to live up to family responsibilities...a little sugar went a long way. He veered left, away from the produce. "Does your mom like flowers?"

"I guess." Jordan bent over a pale blossom, inhaling deeply. "This one smells nice."

"Don't your mom's boyfriends ever bring her flowers?"

Jordan snorted. "Boyfriends? My mom doesn't have any boyfriends."

"Now? Or ever?"

"Ever."

Interesting. "She never goes out on dates or anything?"

"Mom says she's got enough on her plate without adding the trouble of a man to her life."

"Trouble, huh?" Finn dismissed a pot of orange flowers, purple orchids on their long, curvy sticks and fuzzy violets. Amelia's lack of male companionship could have been a contributing factor to her willingness to...help him...when she'd arrived on her mission with the specimen cup last fall. Maybe she only got involved when she was out of Jordan's sight, not wanting her daughter to know about it.

His brother Derek kept any meaningless dating he did well off his kids' radar, not wanting them to be hurt. Or get the wrong idea.

"What about these?" Finn held up a bunch of bright yellow lilies. "Think your mom would like these?"

Jordan nodded. "Yes. They're pretty."

"Good." He reached across her and lifted a cellophane-wrapped bouquet of the pale pink roses from the tall vase. "And these—" he handed them to her "—are for you."

"For me?" A faint blush the same color as the flowers appeared in her cheeks. She glanced at the floor, a small smile playing on her lips. "Th-thanks. No one's ever given me flowers before. Well, Joey Greenwald gave me some dandelions when we were in first grade, but that doesn't count."

"Joey Greenwald better mind his manners around—" the words got stuck but Finn forced them out "—my girl, or he'll have to answer to me. Dandelions. What was he thinking?"

Her smile grew larger, and she shifted, her sandals squeaking.

He set the lilies in the basket, reached for Jordan, then abruptly changed his mind, instead commandeering the cart she'd let go of. Basket wobbling because of a faulty wheel—kind of the way he felt at the moment—he headed for the natural food section.

"I think the canned organic pumpkin is around here somewhere."

"Here it is. I found it!" Jordan called from the far end of the aisle. She stood on tiptoe to reach.

The turquoise top she wore rode up in the back as she stretched.

Revealing an ugly purple mark.

"Jordan." He rushed to her side, grabbed the hem of the shirt and lifted it. The mottled mark was the size of a silver dollar. "How the heck did you do this?"

She twisted, looking over her shoulder. "Oh. I bumped into the end of the island the other day. It's just a bruise. I've got plenty of them."

"This is normal?"

She shrugged. "Sometimes."

"Oh, my," a wavering voice said from behind Finn. "That's a nasty looking bruise."

Finn turned to face the gray-haired woman, and Jordan pulled the bottom of the shirt from his grasp and tugged it down.

The woman stared hard at Finn, and to his surprise, she shook her head and gave him a wide berth, blue basket tucked on her arm.

"Don't say anything to my mom, okay?" Jordan pleaded. "I'm going to the doctor tomorrow. She doesn't need to know how bad the bruising is again."

"Uhhh...no. While there are certain things your mother might not need to know, when it comes to your health, I will not keep anything from her. No way. I will be asking her about this later so I know what to tell the doctor tomorrow."

"The blood count will confirm it." Jordan sighed as she set the can of pumpkin in the cart. "More transfusions for me."

This time he did pull her into an embrace, placing a kiss on the top of her head. Sometimes it was hard to remember she was so sick.

And other times, it consumed him.

She squirmed in his embrace, so he released her. "No big deal," she mumbled, rearranging the flowers in the cart. "Not like it's the first time."

"It'll be the first time for me," he said. "I think maybe you'll have to hold *my* hand."

"You'll get used to it." One corner of her mouth quirked up as she shrugged.

It tugged at his heart that any kid, let alone *his* kid, had to get used to something like that. But she obviously didn't want to make a big deal about it. He reached for another can of the pumpkin. "Let's get out of here and on to the next activity, huh?"

"What's that?"

"You'll see."

Given her hectic life as a single mom and career woman, Amelia had often longed for quiet alone time.

She should have been more careful what she'd wished for.

The empty house didn't even creak. Sunshine battered the deck off her prison, and if she saw one more fluffy white cloud float by over the lake, she was going to lose it completely.

Rain would be much more to her liking.

She checked the clock on the laptop. Ten minutes later than the last time she'd looked. She flipped through the pages of the *Journal of Chiropractic Medicine*—Sia was forwarding her mail in weekly batches—but couldn't focus. She tossed it to the foot of the bed.

Not a big fan of television, she nonetheless activated the flat-panel screen. Finn's satellite dish delivered over a hundred channels. She surfed through the guide past all of them. Grown men driving around in circles. Grown men almost being washed overboard to catch crab. Grown men paid millions of dollars to stand in the outfield and scratch their crotches, occasionally catching a ball.

No, no, and definitely no.

She shut the TV off. The remote joined the discarded magazine. This boredom made the humiliating sponge bath Finn's RN sister had given her that morning look like a fun day at the spa in comparison.

And it had been only two weeks since Amelia had arrived

to get Jordan. Two lousy weeks.

Only twelve more to go to hit forty weeks of pregnancy.

Maybe she could convince Dr. Hawkins to put her into a drug-induced coma for the rest.

Of course, that would leave Jordan alone with Finn. The man who didn't want to be a dad to a young girl who so desperately wanted one she'd concocted the hare-brained plan that had landed them in this situation.

Amelia could have been stuck at home in her own bed if not for Jordan's adventure. She sighed.

Chip—at some point she'd adopted Finn's ridiculous nickname for the baby—shifted and rolled. The fabric over her stomach poked up, to the right of her belly button. Amelia held her breath. Every time he got rowdy in there now, she worried. Every time he settled down for too long she worried.

The coma idea sounded better and better.

The baby used her already-full bladder as a punching bag—or soccer ball, hard to say—and Amelia gritted her teeth and contracted her muscles. Wetting the bed would add another dimension to the fun and games for the day. "Thanks a heap, Chip. Now I have to go to the bathroom."

She tossed back the sheet, pushed herself up into a sitting position. Black dots swam across her vision. After the dizziness passed, she swung her feet to the floor.

The muscles in her legs protested as she shuffled toward the bathroom. Her right lat muscle spasmed. She dug her knuckles into it.

Medication bottles littered the sink countertop, a minipharmacy. Prenatal vitamins no longer sufficed. Now she also took antinausea meds, stool softeners, plus steroid injections once a week to speed Chip's lung development in case he did put in an early appearance. Antibiotics played a part, as well.

She'd never taken so much as a Tylenol while pregnant before this.

On the way back to bed, she lingered by Finn's dresser and a framed photo of four boys in stair-step order, from shortest to tallest. She suspected Finn was the tallest. Which would make this the four middle boys—Finn, Greg, Hayden and Ian. They wore cutoff jean shorts, mud-splattered T-shirts and broad, mischievous grins. Each crooked his arm around the neck of the boy next to him. The smallest held up a tiny fish on a string.

Amelia ran her fingertip over the word *Brothers* etched into the dark wooden frame at the top. At the bottom "All for one, one for all" was inscribed. Had his childhood actually been as idyllic as this snapshot implied? From what she'd seen of the family so far, the amount of togetherness they still shared, it must have been.

She was consumed with longing. Amelia caressed her belly as she trudged to the far side of the bed. For a moment she pressed her palm against the glass door, heat radiating into her skin. Every once in a while, she spent several hours on a chaise longue on the deck, enjoying the fresh air and sunshine. It was like a tropical vacation, a break from her normal "prison" of Finn's bedroom.

With a sigh, she turned. Sat on the bed. Resumed the flat-on-her-back position and placed her still-warm hand on her stomach. "Feel the sunshine, Chip? Next summer, I promise, I'm taking you and Jordan fishing. I don't know how to fish, but we'll figure it out together."

###

She woke sometime later to wonderful smells from downstairs, mostly unknown, but one distinctly resembling the spices of a pumpkin pie. The sun had moved lower on the horizon. She dragged over her laptop and accessed the kitchen cam. No one appeared in view.

Footsteps clattered on the stairs. Just outside the door, Finn's and Jordan's voices carried on a murmured conversation for several minutes.

"Hey!" Amelia called. "Either come in here or talk louder."

Finn entered carrying a vase of yellow flowers. "We have a surprise for you," he announced.

"I'm not much of a surprise kind of girl," she said, every muscle in her body tensing. The last man who'd announced a surprise had been her so-called husband. His hadn't been a very good surprise. Her stomach started to churn. She clenched her teeth and willed the churning to subside.

"I told you," Jordan said, following him into the room. "Don't call it that."

He glanced down at the vase. "These are for you. They're from Jordan and me."

"No, they're not. They're from you." Jordan waved a bouquet of pink roses. "And look, Mom. Finn got these for me. Aren't they gorgeous?" She crawled onto the bed, sticking the flowers in Amelia's face.

"They're very pretty, honey. I'd appreciate them more if you didn't try to shove them up my nose."

Her child laughed, the sound easing Amelia's stomach.

"Sorry." Jordan pulled them back a few inches. Amelia made admiring noises, inhaling the soft perfume of the blossoms. Score one for the antinausea meds.

Finn rounded the foot of the bed. "Where should I put these?"

"Over there, on the media shelves. Where I'll be able to see them."

He cleared some DVDs off the top shelf, set the vase on it. "How's that?"

"Good. Thank you. They're lovely."

"That's not the surprise."

"It's not?" She flexed her feet beneath the covers, stretching the muscles in her legs that quivered in fight or flight response.

He shook his head. "Now, we need some cooperation from you. Do you trust me, Amelia?"

She glanced at her daughter. The tentative smile on her face overpowered the paleness, the dark circles under her eyes, the tiredness in them. "Say yes, Mom," Jordan urged.

Amelia looked back at Finn. His mischievous grin confirmed it—he was the tallest of the fishing boys in the photo. "I suppose," she finally drawled.

Jordan clapped her hands and scrambled off the bed, bouncing her. Chip started kicking hard.

Finn pulled something out of his back pocket. A navy-blue dish towel. He folded it lengthwise, then held it in front of him as he bent toward her.

"Wait a minute. What are you doing?"

"I'm blindfolding you. We can't very well set up a surprise in the same room as you without a blindfold, can we?"

Jordan paused in the doorway. "Don't be a spoilsport, Mom. We worked hard on this. Come on."

Amelia sighed. "All right."

"Good choice." He draped the cloth over her eyes.

She lifted her head, allowed him to tie the ends at the back of her head. His lips brushed her ear. "Wish I had you in my bed under much different circumstances," he whispered. "Blindfolded. Kinky."

She opened her mouth to respond, then shut it, not knowing where Jordan was.

"One more thing. We don't want you listening, either," he said. "So, we have these." He settled a pair of large headphones over her ears. The crashing roll of waves blended with gentle instrumental music.

Great. Now she was immobilized, blind and deaf. But Jordan's anticipation made Amelia lie there and take it despite her rising anxiety.

The bed jiggled. The air in the room stirred as they flitted around. Tantalizing aromas—non-pumpkin pie ones—got stronger. She sniffed, analyzing. What was it?

A finger tapped the tip of her nose. The left headphone was lifted. "What part of surprise don't you get?" Finn asked. "Do you try to find your Christmas presents before Christmas, too?"

"No. It just smells good—"

"Of course it does. *I* made it."

She scowled. "I was trying to figure out what it was by the smell."

"Well, stop. We need two more minutes. Think you can survive your curiosity that long?"

"If I must."

"Good." He let the earpiece drop against her ear, once

more shutting her out of the room.

She had no way to tell if it was two minutes or ten or something in the middle when he finally removed the headphones completely. The towel also came off.

She opened her eyes, then blinked a few times. A red-and-white checked tablecloth was spread over the empty side of the bed. On it was a platter of fried chicken, a tossed salad and a watermelon elaborately carved into a basket containing a juicy fruit salad.

"What's this?" She nudged a long glass pan filled with...she dipped her finger in it. Sand. A partially buried bowl of water was tucked into the corner.

"That's the beach, Mom. We're having a beach picnic." Jordan hovered at the side of the bed.

"A beach picnic?"

Finn pushed open the glass doors, letting in a blast of warmer air. "Yep. We figured if you couldn't go to the beach, we'd bring the beach to you. Check it out." He picked up the remote from the night table, aiming it at the big screen and turning on the TV. They'd hooked Jordan's video camera to it. The beach, dotted with families under umbrellas, kids running along the edge of the water, appeared—the red-and-white checked tablecloth at the bottom of the frame. The camera jerked and wobbled, going out of focus as he turned it around.

Jordan waggled her fingers. "Hi, Mom! Welcome to beach six on Presque Isle." The girl launched into a travelogue spiel, coached at times by Finn's off-camera, sensual voice.

Amelia's chest tightened. She held out her hand to her daughter. "This is wonderful. Thank you, sweetheart."

Jordan carefully settled onto the picnic cloth, squeezing her fingers. "It was Finn's idea."

As Amelia opened her mouth to thank him, her stomach growled loudly. She pressed her palm to it, face warming.

Finn laughed. "I think that was Chip saying enough with the chitchat. Feed me." He took a plate from the media center.

While they indulged in the best fried chicken she'd ever tasted, the video on the flat-screen offered her a guided tour of Presque Isle, alternately narrated by Jordan and Finn. She saw the Perry Monument, the view of the city from across the bay, and the "floating houses." An otter darted into the bushes after crossing the road. The wild shaking of the camera as Jordan scrambled to capture it made Amelia stop eating and once again give thanks for the antinausea meds. Mallard ducks bobbed on small waves, and turtles sunned themselves on a log.

Sweat dotted Amelia's forehead as warm, sticky air continued to billow in through the open door. "Do me a favor?" she asked Finn, who'd pulled a chair to the side of the bed. "Shut that door? I think I'd like to enjoy my beach picnic in air-conditioned comfort. Phew, it doesn't get this warm in Caribou except maybe a few days in the dead of summer."

After he got up, he set his plate on the chair. The doors trundled shut. He latched them. "Wimp."

The video continued. Finn excused himself to clean up the food, but left her "beach" and "lake" in the glass pan. Jordan shoved it aside, snuggling into Amelia's side, laying her head against her mother's shoulder.

Amelia caressed her long, silky hair, Jordan's pride and joy. The treatments to this point didn't include any meds that would make it fall out. She'd already expressed dismay about losing it from the chemo that would precede the transplant. But that was a bridge to cross in the future. Within minutes, the girl's breathing evened out, and she dropped into sleep.

When Finn came back, Amelia pressed a finger to her lips. He nodded. "Do you want me to put her in her own bed?" he whispered, pantomiming his message as well.

She shook her head.

He moved to the media center, fiddled with Jordan's camera. The screen filled with static for a moment, then new footage appeared.

An almost deserted beach. A small, lone figure at the water's edge. Jordan, with her jeans rolled up to midcalf, the water covering her feet, then receding. She extended her arms, the wind blowing her hair. Tilting her face to the sky, she spun in a slow circle.

Finn leaned over to whisper in Amelia's ear. "She doesn't know I filmed her. Thought you'd get a kick out of watching her."

As he straightened, Amelia grabbed his hand, squeezing it. "Thank you," she said softly. "This...was very thoughtful of you."

"Enough to make you like surprises?"

"Doubt it."

He leaned back down, cupped the side of her face in his palm. "Pay up."

"W-wha—"

His lips brushed hers, a gentle, easy kiss that sent her pulse racing. She glanced down at Jordan as he pulled away.

"Don't worry, she's asleep." He skimmed his fingertips

over Amelia's cheek. "Remember I told you last night, anything you or Jordan need, I want to help."

"I need shelter. Food. Waiting on hand and foot. And you're providing all that. I don't think a bedroom beach picnic counts as a *need*."

He stood, lifting one broad shoulder. "Sometimes the soul needs more than the basics, Amelia. There's bread, and then there's a homemade garlic oregano sourdough." After a wary glance at the television, he stopped in the archway, about to leave. "I'll be back later with dessert." He eased the door three-quarters shut behind him.

Amelia resumed stroking Jordan's hair, watching her daughter relish the sun and the water on the TV. A weather-worn wooden table came into the frame at the bottom. The camera wobbled, then was set down, still pointed in Jordan's direction. A moment passed, and a large, male hand appeared in front of the lens. The focus adjusted automatically.

There was a message in blue ink on his palm.

Wish you were here.

Butterflies that had nothing to do with Chip flitted in Amelia's stomach, and her whole body tensed.

The hand vanished. A second later, Finn stood in front of the camera, bending over to peer into it. He reached out, made an adjustment, then winked. He turned and dashed down the beach in Jordan's direction, catching the girl up in his arms and spinning her around at the water's edge. Her shrieks of laughter carried to the camera's microphone.

They both staggered a moment, then he draped his arm over her shoulders, pointing toward the camera. He said something, and they both waved.

Susan Gable

Wish you were here.

CHAPTER NINE

FOR A DAY OFF, IT hadn't been much fun, or relaxing. No day at the beach.

With Hayden out on a date and the rest of the house still, Finn stood in Jordan's darkened bedroom. Even in the dim light slanting from the bathroom, he could see the healthier color of her skin.

Thinking about the medical procedures she'd endured to change her pallor to something more normal, he sank to his knees on the braided rug next to the bed. Her left arm lay outside the covers. He skimmed the edge of the bandage in its crook, where they'd drawn blood that morning.

He'd almost drawn blood of his own when the damn inept newbie at the office had stuck her for the third time and still not hit a vein. Jordan had scrunched her eyes shut and squeezed his hand so hard the bones grated. He'd damn near lost the eggs Benedict he'd had for breakfast.

Which would have proven his ineptness as a father. His inability to handle his first major "daddy" task with Jordan. With his daughter.

Amazing what a unit of blood could do. Unfortunately, it turned out that too many transfusions could damage her liver—to the point of failure. Hence the need for the transplant to reboot her own blood cell making system.

He brushed loose hair from her forehead, then awkwardly

leaned over and kissed her. "You'll be the death of me, kiddo, I can see it now."

She stirred, then rolled onto her side. His knees popped as he stood. After one lingering look from the doorway, he headed to check on Amelia.

His admiration for her had grown enormously that morning. To helplessly watch your child suffer through medical procedures...

And she'd been doing it alone.

The television and computer monitor lit her room. Yesterday's video of Jordan on the beach. Amelia jabbed the remote, freezing the image, when he entered.

"You're still awake."

"No, I'm sleeping. I'm just good at multitasking."

"What's keeping you up tonight?"

She sighed, laying her hands on her stomach. "Chip's training for a marathon. Or something."

Finn crossed the room. "May I?" He gestured to the bed.

"Why not?" She grabbed for the covers to pull them up.

"No, don't." He took them from her hands. "Please..." He climbed onto the mattress, sitting beside her with his legs folded. The thin nightshirt draped over her rounded belly shifted as his son moved. Finn gently placed his hand over the spot. The baby bumped his palm repeatedly.

"I see what you mean." Finn leaned over. "Chip, it's bedtime."

"Faulty argument. These days, it's always bedtime for us."

"Okay. It's *night*time. Your mother needs sleep. Settle down in there. You've been a good boy for staying in your room so far, so I'm doubling your allowance." Finn lifted his gaze to meet Amelia's. "Do you think he already knows that twice nothing is nothing?"

"Of course. He's very smart. Advanced for his age."

"Which would explain why he was in such a hurry to get out here." Beneath his hand, the baby's movements slowed. "Well, I'll be damned."

Amelia snorted. "Figures. He likes the sound of your voice."

"He does? So should I keep talking until he falls asleep in there?"

"You don't have to."

"What if I want to?"

"Your choice... I heard you threatened the tech this morning at the doctor's office." Her eyebrows rose slightly.

"Is that who I threatened? I thought I'd threatened an incompetent idiot who couldn't draw blood without making a very stoic girl, who'd assured me all along that it wasn't a big deal and wouldn't hurt much, wince in pain." Finn stroked small, featherlight circles on Amelia's belly.

"Your status has been elevated. First flowers, then threatening bodily harm to people who hurt her. I swear, much more and you're going to bypass fatherhood and be catapulted right to demigod." Amelia sighed, then placed her hand over his to still it. "She's putting you on a high pedestal, Finn."

"And you're worried about what happens when I fall from grace and she finds out I'm only human?"

"Something like that, yeah."

He was worried, too. He'd crashed and burned enough in his life. That fizzing spark, the disappointment in the eyes of someone who loved you, who you loved. He didn't want to experience that again.

He pulled his hand away. "So, what am I supposed to do? Not even try?"

When the silence stretched to the point of making them both fidget, Amelia said, "Change of subject." She picked up the remote, and the video lurched back to life on the TV. A moment later, his hand came into view on the screen.

Finn's face warmed when she paused it again with his ink-covered palm slightly off center. The note had been a crazy impulse. He cleared his throat. "Okay. What about it?"

"What possessed you to write that?"

He shrugged. What *had* possessed him? "Temporary insanity?"

She watched him. Heat crept up the back of his neck. He shrugged again. "It felt like one of those perfect moments, you know?" He reached across her, grabbing the remote from her far hand. He skipped forward to the part where he'd swept Jordan into his arms and spun her.

"See that? That was just amazing. But one thing was missing."

Amelia waited several moments. "What?"

"You."

She closed her eyes and pressed her lips tight.

He shifted, then cradled her cheeks in his hands. "Don't do that, Amelia. Don't shut me out."

If he hadn't been holding on to her, he'd have missed the slight shake of her head. "We can't always get what we want," she whispered. "Please, Finn, don't...it's not fair. I'm trapped here, at your mercy."

He recoiled. "At my *mercy?*" He jumped off the bed,

grabbed the covers and pulled them over her. "If you want, I can make arrangements for you to move to my parents' house. The rest of the Hawkins crew will still take care of you and Jordan until Chip's born, but you won't have to see me at all. I wouldn't want you feeling beholden to me, or anything crazy like that. Or trapped." He strode for the door.

"Wait! That's not what I meant. Damn it. Finn. Come back here. Finn!"

He made it to the door of his temporary bedroom in the front of the house before his cell phone buzzed in his pocket. He yanked it out, checked the caller ID. Amelia. As expected. He shoved it back in his pocket.

Hayden poked his head out of his bedroom on the other side of the hallway. "Everything all right? Thought I heard Amelia."

"You did. Everything's fine."

"Uh-oh."

"Uh-oh, what?"

"Let's have a beer, Fish. I'm buyin'." Hayden came out wearing only a pair of skintight boxer briefs.

"Put some clothes on. There's an impressionable young girl in the house, and she doesn't need to see your abs of steel. Or anything else, for that matter." Finn gestured at his brother. "Besides, I don't see any pockets in that getup if you're buying."

"Sure."

Finn fumbled with the knob on the door at the top of the front staircase. During the remodel, he'd had the door installed, and the top railings replaced with walls. This door and the one in the kitchen that protected the back staircase both had keypad lock systems. To keep his private space private.

His cell phone vibrated against his thigh again.

As he started down the stairs, Hayden caught up to him. In the foyer, they turned right into the bar. Finn flipped on a couple lights. Enough to see by, not enough to blind them, or make anyone think they were open for business. He slumped onto the end stool, head in his hands.

"Uh-huh. I knew it." Hayden slipped behind the bar. His brother had held numerous summer jobs tending bar, and when needed, pinch-hit for Finn at Fresh.

"Knew what, smart guy?"

Hayden got two mugs out of the cooler, tipped one and pulled the Killian handle. Foam sloshed over the edge and trickled down the side when he set it in front of Finn. "You're a goner."

Finn jerked his head up. "Goner? You'd better dump that beer. You've obviously had too much already."

"How long before you suspected about Greg and Shannon?"

"That first time we saw them together, the day he brought her and Ryan home for Sunday dinner."

"I rest my case." Hayden chugged some of the foamy ale, then wiped the back of his hand across his mouth.

"Like I'm going to take relationship advice from you, creator of the patented Thirty Days, No More, No Less Relationship System."

"You just admitted there's a *relationship*."

Finn swore.

###

She'd hurt him. He'd reached out, stepped up to the plate with Jordan, and in return, she'd hurt him.

For the fourth time, Amelia stabbed the redial button on her cell. His phone rang. And rang. Normally he answered her calls by the second ring, even when he was busy in the kitchen. After five rings, it went to his voice mail.

She hung up without leaving a message.

And stewed.

Five more minutes passed. Then ten. When she dialed again and he still didn't answer, she pushed herself upright, swung her legs off the bed. If the mountain wouldn't come to her...

Outside her room, she paused for a quick peek into Jordan's. The familiar sight of her daughter sleeping peacefully took Amelia's tension down a notch.

She had no idea which of the other bedrooms Finn had moved into or which one belonged to his brother Hayden. She crept down the hall, trying doors.

To no avail. Though she found their rooms, neither of them was there. Where the hell was Finn?

Amelia hesitated by the door to the front stairs. She cupped her belly protectively. That would be pushing her luck way too far.

Then stairs creaked.

She froze as the door opened and Finn appeared, his brother at his shoulder.

"Amelia! What the hell are you doing out of bed?" Finn closed the gap between them in a single stride.

"Don't forget what I said," Hayden called.

Finn saluted him with one finger.

Before she knew what was happening, he'd swung her into his arms and was carting her down the hall. "You wouldn't answer my calls. I needed to talk to you."

"You're risking the lives of both *your* children to talk to me? The ogre who's holding you captive?"

"You're not an ogre." She sighed. "You misunderstood what I was saying. And I wasn't up that long. It was like two bathroom trips."

He eased her onto the bed. She grabbed for his arms. "Please stay and listen to me."

He peeled her fingers from his forearms, then tucked the covers tightly around her. He sat on the edge of the bed beside her. "I don't appear to have a choice. I'm not going to play any part in your breaking Bethany's rules."

"I'm sure you've broken a rule or two."

"Not when my daughter's life...my son's life...depended on it."

"*My* daughter. *My* son."

"Right. I'm just the sperm donor with temporary daddy privileges. Make sure I don't ever forget that, huh?" The muscle at his jaw twitched.

"Best that you do remember. Best that Jordan remembers, too. You said it yourself, you're not ready to be a dad."

"Maybe I could get ready." His shoulders drooped. Pain, mingled with hope, flickered in his eyes. Like a basset hound at the pound.

Which was why she never visited the pound.

He blew out an exasperated breath tinged with the yeasty scent of dark beer. Her mouth watered. She didn't have one often, but it was nearly a year since she'd indulged in an after-work brew with Sia. And it would be months more before she could again.

"Damn it." She latched on to his arms and yanked, drawing him down. When he leaned over her, she threaded one hand into his thick hair.

"Amelia," he murmured, "what are you doing?"

"Kiss me. Please..."

He groaned. "Woman, you are insane."

"Probably. Damn pregnancy hormones."

He let her drag his head the rest of the way down. Let her take the lead. Heat spiraled through her as they kissed. Her pulse raced. He was ale and passion...and everything forbidden to her.

Only when a demanding ache began to throb between her thighs did she push him away.

He drew in a ragged breath, resting his forehead against hers. "I like the way you kiss and make up," he murmured.

"Mmm...gives an all new meaning to kiss the cook."

"Hey. I'm a chef, not a cook."

"Tomato, to-mah-to."

"You like to piss me off, don't you?" He eased upward, the corners of his mouth twitching.

"Apparently it's a gift I possess."

"No kidding."

"Seriously, Finn. I'm sorry about earlier. I didn't mean to sound ungrateful for all the things you're doing for me. For Jordan." Amelia fussed with her hair, straightening it. "But try to put yourself in my place."

"You don't like to need help. I get that."

"It's more than that." She closed her eyes. "You scare me.

Not because you're an ogre," she quickly added. "I don't like feeling...vulnerable."

When he didn't answer, she opened her eyes again. His brows were drawn down in a frown.

"Let's just say that I'm wary of toads in prince clothing," she stated. "For good reason. And leave it at that, huh?" She didn't like to talk about the man who'd charmed and seduced her into a con marriage that turned out to be as fake as he'd been. Jordan had no idea. Sia didn't either. Amelia's dirty little secret, one she preferred to keep buried.

"So, I'm not an ogre, I'm a toad? Is that why you just kissed me? To see if I'd turn into a prince?"

"That's just it, Finn. There's no such thing as a prince. Only toads pretending to be princes."

"Nice to know that I'm just one toad of many, then. Or was there one particular toad...?"

"There was."

"Ah." Finn brushed his fingers over her cheek again. "If I ever meet this guy, I have a cleaver with his name on it. They'll never find the body when I get done with it. What exactly is his name again? I forget."

She smiled. The idea had appeal, she had to admit. The police had never found him. Neither had the P.I. she'd hired when the police turned their attention elsewhere.

If not for deciding to spend her money, once she'd had some again, on better things—like donor sperm, artificial insemination and Jordan—she'd probably still be obsessed with finding the bastard.

But she'd come up with a much better plan for her life. "Thanks," she said. "But he's not worth dulling your knife over."

"Wrong. He made you afraid of me." Finn cupped her face. "I'm not perfect, Amelia. Far from it. But I won't hurt you. Abandon you. Smack you around." He watched her intently as he presented the options. "Whatever he did, I'm not him."

She turned her head, pressed a kiss to his palm, but didn't answer.

Finn lay flat on his back, staring up at the ceiling in his darkened bedroom. Though he'd been in the position only a short time, he already wanted to roll over.

His appreciation for Amelia and her situation deepened. He'd never met a more amazing woman. Smart, funny, independent...and able to arouse him with a single kiss.

She'd blown his mind by initiating that kiss. Just when he thought he knew where he stood with her, she surprised him.

The attraction they were forbidden to act upon was still mutual.

And damned frustrating.

He'd left her room and hit the shower. He'd turned the water cold.

Now, as was his habit, he reviewed plans for the next day's menus as he lay there. But an image kept intruding upon his thoughts. Jordan, her pale face lined with pain, her eyes scrunched shut, his heart pounding and palms slick with sweat as he held her hand.

After his second marriage had failed, he'd accepted that he'd be a career guy and leave the family stuff to his siblings, content to be Uncle instead of Daddy.

But now there was Jordan. And Chip.

And Amelia. A smile on his lips, Finn drifted to sleep...

With the restaurant put to bed for the night, Finn climbed the U-shaped back staircase to the second floor. The wall between the first and second landings was lined with framed pictures, visual reminders of why he worked so damn hard. In ascending order, they chronicled his and Amelia's life together.

Their wedding a year after he'd graduated from culinary school.

Jordan's birth a year after that, and subsequent christening, surrounded by the Hawkins family, after Amelia and he moved back to Erie from New York City when their daughter was two months old.

The ribbon-cutting ceremony in front of Amelia's new practice.

Jordan's first day of kindergarten, and a circular frame containing all her school pictures through this year's eighth-grade photo.

The last few pictures were the grand opening of Fresh, three years ago, and the ultrasound image that constituted their son's first photo.

Pulling his T-shirt over his head as he entered the master bedroom, he dropped it into the laundry basket just inside the door. Strong scents, like the ones that clung to his clothes after a night of cooking, bothered Amelia this pregnancy. He tossed his pants into the basket as well.

His eyes adjusted to the darkness. The drapes over the

sliding glass doors stirred with the night breeze...and their bed was empty.

"Amelia?" He stepped out onto the deck.

She turned from the railing. The gossamer cotton nightgown she wore caressed every pregnancy-enhanced curve. With a wicked you're-about-to-get-lucky smile that made his heart hammer, she began to undo buttons.

When the last one was undone, she slid the fabric down her shoulders, letting it drop at her feet.

The wind fanned her hair.

He already ached with need. "Love the outfit."

"Words are cheap, hotshot."

His boxers hit his ankles a second later, the cool night air doing nothing to kill his very obvious arousal. "Proof enough?" He stepped out of his underwear and started toward her, dodging the chaise longue.

She shivered as he lowered his mouth to her collarbone. He warmed her flesh with his breath, then stroked her with the tip of his tongue. He grazed his teeth over the sensitive skin, and she shivered again.

He took her breast into his mouth.

She moaned, threading her fingers through his hair and holding him there. When he had her squirming, he sank to his knees. He knew just where and how to touch her, to please her.

The second time she lifted her face, panting his name and crying out her satisfaction, he pulled her toward the chaise longue. He sat on the end, leaning back on his elbows to make room for her.

She straddled him, guiding him home.

As she took him into her welcome warmth, he decided home was the exact right word for it.

Rational thought fled as she made love to him.

When their appetites had been sated, he looked up at her flushed face, her hair wind-blown. "Have I mentioned recently how much I love you?"

She smiled. "Why, no, I don't believe you have."

He sat up, wrapping his arms around her. "I love you, Dr. Amelia Young. I'll never let you down."

Finn woke early the next morning with a hard-on that wouldn't quit.

Another cold-shower morning.

Shaved, showered and thoroughly frustrated, he crept down the back staircase, running his fingers along the wall between the landings.... and ground to a halt.

He stared, remembering the framed photographs along this wall in his dream.

He shook his head.

Sex dreams were one thing. But he'd created an entire family life with Amelia and Jordan.

"I'll never let you down."

He'd made similar promises, in reality, to his ex-wives.

Look how those had turned out.

CHAPTER TEN

JUNE STUTTERED INTO JULY. Amelia kept marking X's on the calendar on her laptop. She'd spent twenty-six nights in Finn's bed. Alone.

The Internet became her main playground.

She'd never had quite this much free time to spend surfing.

Ever since the night she'd gotten out of bed to chase him down—the night they'd "kissed and made up"—Finn had been skittish. He never made her wait more than two rings before he picked up her calls, but he kept his distance.

Like he wasn't completely sure just how to handle her.

Which made two of them. She didn't know how to handle him, either.

Amelia scowled at Finn's sister, Elke, as she practically floated across the bedroom from the bathroom, a dreamy smile on her face.

This morning, Elke had been preoccupied during the entire ritualized humiliation called a sponge bath, and while that suited Amelia—although humiliated beat smelly—now her curiosity got the better of her. "What's with you this morning? Pregnant women aren't supposed to do drugs. Not the kind that makes you smile like that, anyway."

The nurse's cheeks reddened. "What? I can't smile?"

"Come on, you know the deal. You're living for both of us

right now." The pair had bonded quickly—not only because Elke provided her essential, considerate care, but because of their shared pregnancies. Elke was two weeks ahead of Amelia, and was also carrying a boy.

The woman's blush deepened.

"Oh, hell's bells." Amelia sighed. "That's just wrong, coming in here with your I-got-lucky-this-morning glow. Some of us aren't allowed to get lucky."

"Sorry." Elke flashed a quick grin. "I don't think it's a coincidence that hormones and horny are such similar words."

Amelia groaned. "At least you can do something about it."

"You don't want the details, do you?"

Amelia put her fingers in her ears and hummed.

Elke burst into laughter. "I'm kidding. Really. Sorry. I'll try to take my contentment down a notch."

"Thanks. I'm jealous enough that you get to do everything else I can't."

Elke changed the bed linens one half at a time, making Amelia shift from side to side.

As she was finishing, the door swung open and Jordan staggered in, loaded down with a pair of boxes. "Mom, this stuff came for you. Maybe one of them is my dress for the wedding?"

"Oh, good. Bring them over here." Amelia checked the return addresses, pulling out the small box from the eBay seller. She'd been surprised by Shannon's "rules" of the wedding—all clothes had to be rented or secondhand. But it had handily lent itself to spending hours with her daughter, pouring over eBay in search of the perfect dress for her. The wedding was only days away. "Here it is, baby. Why don't you run into the bathroom and try it on?"

"Yes," Elke said. "Model it for us."

"Okay." Jordan took the box from Amelia and hustled to the bathroom.

Amelia had Elke open the other box for her. She'd had a field day, searching the Internet for unusual gifts to give her personal chef. It wasn't like she could run out to the store, and she desperately wanted to show him a little appreciation. At least he'd given up on fighting her over the room and board checks.

After pawing through the brown paper used as filler, Finn's sister cooed. "Awww. Is this for anyone I know?" She held out the black apron that said Kiss the Cook in bold red letters.

"You know any cooks?"

"Call Finn a cook and you'll be lucky to get peanut butter and jelly sandwiches out of him." Her eyes widened. She cocked her head. "Ohhh, wait a minute. Now I get it. You've been kissing the cook, haven't you? And can't get lucky. And that's why you're so cranky."

Amelia's face warmed.

"You're blushing!"

"No. I have not been kissing the cook." Not lately, anyway. The fact that she missed doing so was none of Elke's business. "And keep your voice down. I don't want Jordan to hear you talking like that."

"Why not? Isn't it the best thing that could happen? You and Finn share one-point-five children right now. Two children soon enough, so—"

"Speak for yourself, 'soon enough.' The end of this pregnancy can't come soon enough for me."

Elke propped her fists on her hips. "What's wrong with a little kissing between people who have kids together?"

"Nothing can come of it, that's what."

"Not right now, but later..."

"I'm not talking about sex. I'm talking about something more between Finn and me." She lifted her shoulders. Not willing to share her secret hurts and fears, she opted for a convenient excuse. "My life is nine hundred miles away. Your brother's life is here."

"Oh, people work that stuff out all the time. You're just—"

Jordan opened the bathroom door a crack. "Mom, I can't tie this."

Amelia was halfway upright before she realized what she was doing.

"I'll help," Elke said, hurrying to the bathroom.

With a sigh, Amelia slumped back against the pillow. Great. She'd managed to buy the dress for her daughter, but couldn't even help her get into it.

Hayden walked in, a large black object in one hand. "Morning. Saw the door was open and assumed you were now receiving visitors."

Jordan came out of the bathroom hesitantly. "Well? How does it look?" She did a slow twirl.

The dress had a black halter top and a white skirt with black embroidered flowers at the hem, which hit just below Jordan's knees.

The top showed off the fact that her baby wasn't a baby anymore. At some point during the commotion of the last year, her little girl had transformed into a teenager.

And Amelia had missed it. Her nose tingled. "Very pretty, sweetheart."

"You'll be the most beautiful girl there," Hayden said. He set whatever he was carrying on the floor, and moved to take Jordan's hands. "You'll dance with me, right?"

"What will your date say?" Jordan giggled as Hayden lifted her hand to guide her in a circle.

"I don't have a date for the wedding."

"You don't?" The note of incredulity in Amelia's voice made her bite her tongue. But women seemed to eat out of Hayden's hand. Even Jordan had a little crush on him, hanging on his every word.

"Finished things with Teresa last week. Besides, women get funny ideas if you take them to a wedding. Never a good plan."

Elke, who'd followed Jordan from the bathroom, gave her younger brother a sharp look. "He doesn't even bring a girl home for Sunday dinner, Amelia, never mind a wedding."

He flashed her a cocky grin. "Hell, no. Again, women expect things if you take them to meet your family. There are rules about this sort of stuff." He drew Jordan closer. "So I'll dance with this woman and make all the other guys jealous."

Jordan stumbled, then backed out of his embrace, eyes down. "Mom, can I go show Finn?" On the kitchen cam he was puttering away over the stove, even though it was Monday and Fresh was closed. Some men retreated to a workshop, Finn hid out in the kitchen on his day off.

"Sure, baby." Amelia picked up the apron. "Take this with you. Tell him it's a present from me."

Jordan took it and fled, giving Hayden a shy glance as she

passed him.

"Don't you let my girl down, Hayden Hawkins." Amelia shook a finger at him. "She's already got a crush on you."

His mouth opened a fraction, his eyes widening. "What?" His eyebrows drew together. "Nah. I'm her uncle."

"I'll see that he doesn't," Elke said, folding her arms.

He bent and picked up the black thing off the floor. "Before you both decide to flay me, I brought a present, too. Something I think you're going to love."

"What's that?"

"This is a back-massage chair mat. I found it in my closet last night, and I got to thinking. What if we lay this on the bed? I'll bet your back muscles are killing you by now."

"You're a genius. Let's try it." Amelia closed her computer and moved it out of the way.

Finn set the knife down, wiped his hands on his apron. "Wow. Just wow." He made a circle with his finger. "Turn around, let me see the rest."

The partially bare back of the dress made him press his lips together.

"Well?" Jordan looked at him eagerly. "What do you think?"

"I think you're beautiful." The dress, on the other hand, he wasn't so sure about. Crap. He was thinking like a dad again.

He'd found himself slipping into the role more and more, despite his misgivings. Despite Amelia's misgivings—and threats.

Jordan smiled. "Thanks. I still have to figure out what

shoes I'm wearing and all that, but I really like the dress."

"That's good."

"Oh, I almost forgot. Mom said to give you this. It's a present from her." She shoved something into his hands and headed for the stairs. "I'm going to go hang this up. But I'll be back to help you, if that's okay?"

"Of course it is." She'd taken to spending about an hour with him in the morning, while he did prep work for the day. He'd taught her to crack eggs one-handed, how to make a roué, and she'd mastered the family recipe for triple chocolate brownies. She often made those on her own for the restaurant, where Finn served them with homemade vanilla ice cream and raspberry sauce.

As she flounced up the stairs, he unfolded Amelia's gift.

Kiss the Cook, huh? Insult, or an invitation? He bit back a grin.

He adjusted the laptop on the island shelf, but she didn't have her computer on so he could talk to her. The mounted camera Hayden had installed still ran most of the time, but he couldn't communicate through it. He untied the apron he had on over his jeans, put on Amelia's gift. Water splashed as he tossed some potatoes into a pot for the new gnocchi recipe he was experimenting with. Then he headed upstairs.

The wall between the two landings still seemed mockingly bare, a reminder that fantasy and reality weren't even in the same universe. He finished the climb slowly.

"Ohmigod, ohmigod!" Amelia moaned.

Heart pounding, Finn hurtled the final steps two at a time.

"That feels so good."

Finn halted outside her door.

"Genius. Total genius. Hayden, I love you," Amelia confessed.

Finn burst into the room. "What the hell..." He trailed off as Elke and Hayden, seated on the couch—Elke's bare feet in Hayden's lap while he massaged them—both stared at him like he'd lost his mind.

Which he probably had.

In the bed, Amelia, her body shifting slightly beneath the covers, closed her eyes with a contented sigh.

"...is going on in here?" Finn finished.

Hayden laughed. "Massages. Haven't I told you? The way to a woman's heart, whether she's your sister or not, is through massage."

Elke kicked him in the thigh. "Shut up and rub."

"Watch where you're kicking. I'm fond of nearby anatomy." He dug his thumb into her arch, causing her to slump back onto the brown pillows.

"Be careful where you put pressure," Amelia murmured. "There are points in the feet that have been used by acupuncturists to induce labor. I've actually had some luck with acupressure in a few of my patients who went past their due dates."

"Well, we don't need labor right now, that's for sure. For either of us." Elke draped her arm over her face.

Hayden gave Finn a grin that said he knew all too well what had been going through his brother's mind when he'd heard Amelia moan. He raised an eyebrow. "Nice apron."

Amelia opened her eyes. "Oh. You're wearing it."

Finn crossed to the near side of the bed, the side she didn't usually lie on. "I am. It was supposed to be for your eyes only.

I didn't realize Elke was still here. Or Hayden, either."

Under the covers, Amelia's body undulated, from her upper torso down to her waist. He heard a faint motorized whir and cocked his head. "What *is* happening? I know Chip can be rambunctious, but he doesn't move like that."

"It's a massage pad. Hayden brought it for me."

"Is that...safe?" He looked over at Elke, who still covered her face with her arm. "Elk?"

"Huh? Oh. It's fine. She's not upright, it's not putting any pressure on her cervix. I wouldn't overdo it, but it shouldn't be a problem. Mmm, Hayden, I take back every mean thing I ever said about you. Jeremy has a thing about feet. He won't touch them."

"This is a one-time opportunity. So enjoy it."

"This is part of your breakup dates, isn't it? You lull women into absolute relaxation, then you dump them and cut out before they can think straight."

Hayden laughed. "No, but it's not a bad idea."

Finn glared at him, clearing his throat. Elke dropped her arm and opened her eyes. He jerked his head toward the door.

"Huh? Oh. Hayden...um...I hate to make you stop, but there are a couple of errands I have to run for the wedding, and I could use some help."

"I don't do wedding crap—ow!" Hayden rubbed his thigh where their sister had dug in her heel. "Right. Let's go."

When Elke had gathered her sneakers and socks, she left. Hayden lingered in the doorway for a moment, looking from Amelia to Finn, then he pivoted and left.

Finn sat on the edge of the bed.

Amelia pressed a button on the wired remote in her hand,

and all movement stopped. She exhaled slowly.

"Better?"

She nodded. "You have no idea."

"Thank you for the apron. You didn't have to."

"No, I didn't. That's what makes it a gift." She toyed with the string he'd tied in the front. "How is it you make an apron, of all things, look sexy?"

Warmth surged through him. "You like it, huh?"

"I do." She sighed. "I shouldn't. But I do."

"So are you going to?" He leaned forward.

"To what?"

He pointed to the red words on the apron's bib. "Kiss the cook?"

She smiled. "Thought you were a chef."

He studied her for a moment, then burst out laughing. "You are an evil, evil woman."

"No. Just a woman."

"You're not *just* anything."

"You don't know me. And you're not exactly seeing me at my best here."

"You've spent almost a month in my bed. Under very trying circumstances. I know enough. I'd probably be blinded by sheer amazement if I saw you at your best."

"Am I seeing you at your best?" She curled her fingers around his biceps, toyed with the sleeve of his white T-shirt.

Distracted as he was by her touch, it took a while before he nodded. "Pretty much. I'm normally not this attentive. Too busy. Then again, this is the first time I've ever lived with a woman. Outside of my two wives, I mean. Although...I think I've spent more time with you in a month than I did with them in all the months we were married."

"Hence your divorces."

"Yeah. They both needed a lot more than I could give back then." The fantasy life of his dream came back to him. The long-term marriage to Amelia, raising Jordan with her. Being a real family, not a pretend, short-term father. Did he want more than *she* could give? Were it not for the unexpected twist of fate that had landed her in his bed, she'd have been long gone.

And he'd have been long forgotten, he suspected. Maybe not by Jordan.

But Amelia would have gone on with her own life. Nine hundred miles away.

And he'd have gone on with his, pouring everything he had, all his time, all his efforts, into the restaurant. Alone.

He shivered.

"Someone walk over your grave?" she asked.

"Maybe."

###

"There's no texting in baseball."

Jordan's fingers paused over her phone. She glanced up at Finn, who sat next to her at Jerry Ute Park. "What?"

"Never mind. You're too young to get the reference, I suppose. Who're you texting?"

"Shelby."

"Dumb question." He tapped the brim of the cap he'd bought her first thing at the SeaWolves game. "You bored?"

"Umm..." She was, but he'd given up his Monday night off—time he usually spent experimenting with new dishes—so they could go to a ballgame with some of the family. Uncle Derek and his three kids, Uncle Greg and Ryan, and Uncle Hayden had shown up towing Nick, a cousin she'd never met before.

Also thirteen, he had dark brown hair, familiar blue eyes, and like Finn, a single dimple that appeared when he smiled. His nose seemed a little big for his face, but then...so did hers. She'd snapped Nick's picture and fired it off to Shelby. Maybe her BFF would stop drooling over her father and start drooling over a cousin. That was way less weird.

"I'm going to take that as a yes." Finn sighed. "Guess you're not much of a baseball fan, huh?"

Jordan shrugged. "Guess not. But...I'm glad you brought me. Thanks."

"You're welcome." He lowered his voice. "Truth is, I'm not such a fan myself. But I've never had the chance to be included in a dads-and-kids outing with my brothers. So thank *you*." He patted her arm. He went back to watching—or pretending to watch, now she wasn't so sure—the game. She went back to texting Shelby.

The crack of bats against balls, the cheering—or jeering—of the crowd, the smells of hot dogs and nachos made it an interesting change of pace. Two rows below them, a young couple kept stealing kisses between at-bats. Not disgusting public pawings, but sweet. Like they were in love.

Over in the next section, a guy with a scraggly beard who'd obviously had too many beers yelled at the umpires. Security showed up a few minutes later and escorted the guy from his seat. His neighbors applauded.

At some point, Katie and Lila, Uncle Derek's two girls,

started whining that they were hungry. Ryan and Jack quickly agreed. Finn and Uncle Hayden volunteered to make a concessions run.

Leaving Jordan alone with Nick. Or near enough, anyway. She moved over one seat. "You're Ian's son, right? Finn's my dad, but I only met him, like, a month ago."

Nick turned his attention from the field to look at her. "Really? My dad died when I was a baby. I don't remember him at all."

"What happened to your father? I've asked about him, but no one wants to tell me. Especially Uncle Hayden."

"Unk's cool. He does all kinds of stuff with me...My dad needed a bone marrow transplant." Nick eased closer to her. "Uncle Derek was supposed to be the donor. But my dad got sick with something else before they could do the transplant. I think he had the flu or something like that." He shrugged. "It's not a secret. I'm not sure why they wouldn't tell you."

Jordan gripped the armrests of the seat. Tiny black dots swam across the ball field. The back of her neck felt sweaty. She flung herself forward, sticking her head between her knees the way Aunt Elke had taught her.

Uncle Ian had died waiting for a bone marrow transplant. No wonder none of them would talk to her about it.

"You all right?" Nick patted her awkwardly on the back. "Don't hurl, huh? These are new sneakers."

"Jordan?" Finn's voice carried from a distance. Footsteps pounded down the stairs. Shoving the food at Nick, Finn sank into the seat next to her, an arm around her shoulders. "Jordan?"

She waved a hand at him. "I'm okay." She slowly sat up,

using his arm for balance. A few black dots reappeared, but not as many.

"What the hell happened?" Finn demanded of Nick.

The boy shrugged. "I dunno. One minute we were talking, and the next, she bent over like that."

"Hey, we're trying to watch the game here," said a man from behind them.

"And I'm trying to make sure my kid's not about to keel over, buddy, so how about you watch your damn game?"

"Take it easy, Finn," Uncle Hayden soothed him. "Getting into a brawl isn't going to help."

"Jordan? Do you want to go home?"

"Yes." She took a deep breath. "Why didn't anyone tell me that Uncle Ian died waiting for a bone marrow transplant? Did he have aplastic anemia, too? Is that why I got it? You should have told me!"

Finn's face paled. Uncle Hayden slumped in his seat.

"All right," Finn finally said. "We'll talk about it." He glanced warily at the guy behind them who'd yelled. "But not here. Derek, Greg, Hayden...a word with you guys, please?"

The four brothers held a quick conference at the top of the stairs, out of earshot of the kids.

"What's aplastic anemia?" Nick asked.

"A blood disease. I need a bone marrow transplant, too."

"So, like...you could die?"

She mostly tried not to think about it. Her baby brother was on the way, with the cells she needed for a cure. Though she understood her low white blood cell count could leave her open to infection, she'd never imagined catching something else and dying before she could have her transplant. Until now.

"Yeah. I could die."

The sounds of the crowd and the sharp crack of a ball being hit filled the long silence that followed. Nick finally said, "That sucks."

"Tell me about it."

"What the hell do I tell her?" Panic drove Finn to pace along the wall while his brothers watched. Once more he was in over his head. Fantasy fatherhood included ball games with your kid. Not explaining to a sick child how your brother had died in a similar situation. "You." He stabbed his finger at Greg. "You're the expert at dealing with this stuff."

"If by *stuff* you mean seriously ill children, then yeah, I have more experience than you do."

"So what do I say? I mean, I don't want to freak her out."

"Newsflash," Derek said. "She's already freaked out."

"You tell her the truth," Greg said. "You lay out the facts about Ian's death from an infection his body just couldn't handle because of his illness. You point out that he had leukemia, which is *not* what she has. And you remind her how important it is to focus on the positive. To fight the good fight."

"And remind her how damn important it is that she tell someone if she's suddenly feeling worse than normal, whatever her normal is. And not keep it a secret." Hayden dragged his hand through his hair.

They all turned to him. "It wasn't—" Greg began.

"—your fault," he, Derek and Finn finished together.

Hayden stared out over the ball field. "Whatever." He cleared his throat. "Just make sure the kid knows to tell someone, okay?"

"Okay." Finn cuffed Hayden lightly on the shoulder.

"Mostly, you tell her how much you love her, and how much faith you have that everything is going to work out for her," Greg said.

Tell Jordan he loved her? Finn started pacing again.

"Welcome to fatherhood," Derek said. "It's not all ball games and hot dogs, is it?"

"No. It sure as hell isn't."

CHAPTER ELEVEN

THEY'D TURNED HER ROOM into wedding central.

Once more Amelia chided herself. She'd wanted more excitement, a change of scenery, but this wasn't exactly what she'd had in mind.

The overwhelming chatter of seven women, crammed into her room and in various stages of dress, mixed with the scent of the flowers and varieties of perfume, made her queasy.

The antinausea meds worked, but Amelia feared they were pushing her luck.

There'd been much laughter early on about how stunned the guys had been last night when the women had busted their bachelor party. For the second wedding in a row, they'd successfully kidnapped the groom—apparently a Hawkins family tradition—to prevent him from being too hungover on his wedding day.

Each bridesmaid wore a different secondhand black dress, chosen to flatter her figure.

Shannon's dress was a simple, knee-length, curve-hugging taffeta, with a stand-up collar shrug. Perfect for a casual outdoor, Sunday afternoon wedding.

It reminded Amelia of the dress she'd worn. She shivered.

Lydia Hawkins draped a single strand of pearls around Shannon's neck. "Something borrowed," she told her soon-to-be daughter-in-law. "My parents gave me these when I graduated from high school."

"I love borrowed." Shannon fingered the necklace, looking at her reflection in the full-length mirror on the back of the bedroom door.

"We know," several of the sisters answered, then they all laughed.

"You owe me a beer," Elke told the others. "I'll collect after this kid is weaned."

"Don't rush it away." Lydia moved to the couch where Elke sat, stocking feet propped up. "They grow up so fast. I mean, here I am, about to watch another one of my babies get married. Seems like only yesterday Greg was born. My hair might be silver, but I don't feel a whole lot older than I did that day. Well...except maybe when it rains."

Jordan came out of the bathroom, Kara behind her. "Mom? What do you think?"

Kara had swept Jordan's hair up in the back, and given her two spiral curls on either side. She wore a hint of pink lipstick and blush...talk about growing up quickly.

Amelia smiled, hoping the quiver in her lower lip didn't show. "You look beautiful, baby." She held open her arms. "Give me a hug."

Jordan shook her head. "You'll mess me up."

"Oh, excuse me. Wouldn't want to do that."

Lydia winked at her.

"What were Finn's weddings like? Did he get married here in Erie?" The questions slipped from Amelia's tongue before her brain engaged.

The chatter in the room dropped to almost nothing, and they stared at her.

"No," Elke said. "Finn eloped both times. Once when he was working in Vegas. You know how they say what happens in Vegas, stays in Vegas?"

Amelia nodded.

"We didn't know he was married that time until he called Cathy and asked her to look at the divorce papers."

"I still say that shows he wasn't serious about them," Lydia said. "If he'd been serious, he'd have brought them home before he married them."

Amelia caught her breath. Her Fake Husband had introduced her to his mother—or at least someone he'd paid to play his mother—the day before their wedding, a very small intimate affair held in the gardens of a local restaurant.

A tidal wave of bad memories stormed her. Chip squirmed, kicking, as a rush of adrenaline flooded her body.

At the fountain ahead, Ron, looking dashing in his black dress suit, and the justice of the peace waited for her. The cement sidewalk through the rose bushes still showed traces of the morning's showers, but the sun shone brightly now. A good omen.

Still, Amelia hesitated upon seeing her mother, Francine, and the man she'd introduced less than an hour ago as "Uncle" Harry. Amelia had stopped calling the men between stepfathers "uncle" after she'd hit high school and started calling them toads when she wanted to be polite, and far worse when she didn't. Francine and Harry stood alongside the open space to Ron's right.

After witnessing her mother's train wreck relationships, especially with the men she married, Amelia had always vowed never to do this.

But Ron had changed her mind. Reliable. Dependable. Always there when she needed him. Like when she'd sprained her ankle two weeks after meeting him. He'd shown up at her graduation from chiropractic school, more than her mother had managed, and toasted her with champagne when she'd been offered a position with a practice three blocks from her house.

So despite the fact that she'd known him for only three months when he'd proposed, she'd said yes. She wasn't about to let the only prince she'd ever stumbled across get away.

He smiled when he saw her standing at the end of the path, and his whole face brightened. The justice of the peace looked up from his notes and also smiled. So did Ron's mother, beside him. Ron's father had passed on several years ago, and Amelia's...hers had just passed on being a father when her mother had announced her pregnancy.

Ron hadn't wanted anything bigger. This wedding was about them, he'd said. The two of them. Joining together.

Amelia smiled at her groom, then started down the path.

Someone's cell phone chimed. Half the women dug in tiny handbags, checking. It was Shannon who pulled hers out. "Hello? Isn't it bad luck to talk to the bride before the wedding? What? It's just *see* the bride, not talk to her?" Shannon shot them a wide grin. "Checking to make sure I haven't gotten cold feet? I haven't. I told you, I'm never letting you go, pal. You're stuck with me now. How's Ryan?" The bride burst into laughter. "Hey, you're the one who gave him the superhero tie. If he wants to wear it, let him wear it. No. I draw the line at masks. No masks. I don't care if he thinks it's funny." She rolled her eyes. Then her mouth quirked and her voice dropped. "Oh, really? A surprise?"

The rest of the room stifled giggles.

Amelia struggled to breathe. Her heartbeat thudded in her ears. Sweat slicked her palms as the memories got stronger. A surprise...

They'd spent their wedding night at her place. Beyond some clothes and toiletries, he hadn't yet had time to move his stuff in. He'd wakened her with kisses, from the top of her head to the soles of her feet.

Which lead to another round of lovemaking.

And another.

Finally, Ron glanced at the clock. "We'd better get a move on. We have to be at the airport in an hour and the cab will be here any minute. Shit." He slapped his forehead.

Amelia climbed from the bed, stretching languidly. "What's wrong?"

"Nothing wrong, exactly. It's just that I have one more surprise for you."

"You do?" Her suitcase was already packed and sitting near the front door with his, ready for their honeymoon trip to Aruba—one of his wedding surprises.

"Yeah, but I have to pick it up first. Damn, it's going to be cutting it close." Ron kicked away the tangle of covers at his

feet and scrambled to dress, as she did. A horn beeped out front of her apartment building. "There's the cab. Let's go."

He stowed both suitcases in the trunk of the taxi, then opened the door for her. He yanked her into his arms and gave her a long, thorough kiss. "I'll meet you at the gate, okay?"

"Okay."

"Flight 672, nonstop service to Aruba is now boarding at gate 22. Passengers needing assistance and those in first class are invited to board at this time."

Amelia stared at the boarding pass in her hand, then shot from the seat, hoisting her carry-on. She scanned the crowd heading down the hallway.

Hurrying to the pay phones, she dug change out of her wallet. Ron had a cell phone for business, but she wasn't sure he'd have it on him. He was supposed to be on his honeymoon. She dialed. No answer. No answer at her apartment, or his, either.

Hopefully, that meant he was even now getting out of a taxi and rushing into the airport.

"Final call for boarding of flight 672 to Aruba."

Her heart pounding, Amelia rushed to the airline employee as she put down the microphone. "Please...my husband isn't here yet. Can you page him again?"

"Absolutely, Ma'am. Ronald Peterson, wasn't it?"

Amelia nodded, then went back to circling the now-empty gate area, stopping to peer into the distance down the hall-

way.

"Ron, where are you?" Her stomach knotted.

When the attendant closed the door, her chest tightened. She approached the woman at the desk again and handed her the paperwork. "Will you be able to get us on a later flight?"

The woman tapped at her keyboard. "We have a flight later this evening. And it looks like there are some empty seats."

"Okay, thanks."

"Maybe he got tied up in traffic," she said, passing back the papers. "Happens more often than you think. People try to cut it too close, and then there's an accident or something, traffic gets tied up—"

"An accident?" Amelia's pulse pounded. "Oh, no. I hadn't even thought of that. What if he's been in an accident?"

She sat in one of the blue chairs for two more hours, making repeated but unanswered phone calls. She finally left in a cab for home. If something had happened to him, that was where the police would call.

Hours later, she hung up the phone. She'd called every major hospital in the area. Nothing. All she could do was wait.

After four days without any word from Ron, no clues, Amelia stood in front of a teller at her bank. "I'm sorry, ma'am, but this account is overdrawn. Do you have another account with us?"

"What? That's not possible. I deposited my paycheck last

week."

"I can make a printout of recent activity, if you like."

"Yes, please. But for now, let's transfer some funds from my savings account."

"How much?"

"Five hundred dollars." She'd looked into hiring a private investigator to find Ron, since the police seemed unconcerned. *"Maybe he got cold feet just a little too late,"* the detective had joked. Funny guy.

"I'm sorry, Dr. Young. There's only two hundred dollars in that account."

"What? No, something's obviously wrong. You must have the wrong accounts. Dr. Amelia Young."

"Ma'am, I have the name right. I have the account numbers right. There's only two hundred dollars in your savings."

Amelia's hands trembled. She gripped the edge of the teller's counter. *"Last week there was over ten thousand in there."*

And now it was gone.

Along with her husband.

The café au lait walls of Finn's bedroom closed in. Female voices and laughter blurred together, a cacophony of sounds that made her head swim. Sweat trickled down the edge of her face. Tightness in her chest made breathing hard.

Amelia grabbed her cell phone, punched in Finn's name, and texted: SOS.

\#\#\#

Finn pulled on his tux jacket, fighting a grin as Greg rose to his feet beside Ryan, tucking the black mask into his back pocket. The crestfallen boy jabbed the toe of his dress shoe into the leg of the bed. Michael Hawkins patted his grandson's shoulder.

"We can still make a break for it, man," Hayden said to Greg, straightening his bow tie as he checked himself out in the dresser mirror. "Runaway grooms are all the rage, I hear. As your best man, it's my job to present all your options."

Greg narrowed his eyes and shook his head. "No way. I almost lost her once. I'm not taking any more chances. I want a ring on her finger."

Finn's cell phone vibrated in his pocket. He pulled it out...

And nearly dropped it. He was out the door and halfway down the hall before anyone else could react.

"You're not the groom," Hayden shouted at his back. "Where the hell are you going?"

Footsteps thudded behind him.

Finn burst into the room, which looked like one—or more—of his sisters' closets had exploded. "You're all decent, right?" He walked straight to Amelia, pushing through a cluster of his startled sisters.

Amelia was breathing heavily, and her eyes were closed. Seeing the pallor of her skin, he grabbed her clammy hand and sat beside her. "Amelia? What's wrong?" He cautiously gathered her in his arms. "You're shaking like a leaf."

He glanced over his shoulder, easing her back onto the bed. "Bethany? Put the damn makeup down and get over here! Something's wrong."

Elke levered herself from the sofa, grabbing something

from the night table and crawling across the bed.

Bethany whacked him on the shoulder. "Get out of the way."

Amelia grabbed his lapels. "No, please. Don't make a big deal. I feel so ridiculous," she whispered. "It's just...I've been in this room alone for five weeks now. And all these people...it's too much."

Elke peeled Amelia's right hand off his tux, fastening a BP cuff around her upper arm. "Lie still. You look like crap."

"Gee, thanks."

"Clear the room, people," Finn ordered. "Grab all your stuff and get out. There are two empty rooms on the left side of the hallway. The guys are in my new room, so you can't use that."

"No, we're not. We're here, too," Hayden said. "What's going on?" A wall of black tuxedos crowded the doorway, with Alan, Derek, Kyle and their dad all crushed into the space around Hayden.

Amelia groaned and closed her eyes again. Bethany grabbed hold of his ear and yanked.

"Ow!" He dropped Amelia's hand and jumped off the bed, bumping into the bedside table, making the lamp sway. With his back pressed against the sliding doors, he rubbed his ear furiously. "What happened to do no harm?"

"You're not my patient. She is," Bethany snapped.

"BP's elevated, 155 over 98." Elke took the stethoscope from her ears. Velcro ripped as she undid the cuff. "Pulse is 120."

"It wasn't that high when I took it earlier."

"For God's sake..." Amelia grabbed the covers and pulled

them over her head. "My blood pressure is high because it's a circus in here!"

"You heard her," Finn told his slack-mouthed family. "Clear out." He checked his watch. "Besides, if I'm not mistaken, we've got a wedding in about twenty minutes."

That did it. The guys scattered first, as the girls gathered up bags and jars and bottles of God-only-knew-what.

Bethany nodded at Elke. "Go ahead. I'll be a few minutes behind you."

Elke passed the stethoscope over. Then she pulled the covers off Amelia's face. "I'll be back before the reception to check on you."

"You won't be the only one," Bethany added.

Elke pulled the bedroom door closed behind her. Silence.

It was then Finn noticed Jordan, face paler than normal despite the makeup she wore, pressed into the corner by the media center. "Hey..." He went to her, curling his palm around her cheek. "Look at you. You're gorgeous."

She smiled shakily.

"What do you say we step into the hall so Bethany can examine your mom?"

"No, wait. Come here, honey."

Bethany shifted out of the way for Jordan. Amelia opened her arms, and her daughter eased into the embrace, sniffling.

"Shhh. I'm fine. Just being a bit silly, is all. Stand up now and let me look at you again." She did.

"You're beautiful. So grown-up." Amelia pressed her hand to her chest. "My little girl's not so little anymore. Have fun at the wedding, okay?"

Jordan nodded. "I'll make videos for you."

"Terrific. We'll watch them together."

"I'll be right out," Finn told Jordan as she passed him on her way to the door.

He glared at his sister. "Mind if I sit down again for a minute? She looks better to me already."

Bethany leaned around him, studying her patient. Amelia gave her a thumbs-up and a sheepish smile. "Really, I'm fine. I'll bet if you took my BP again right now you'd find it's already dropped. I can tell because my heart's not pounding in my ears anymore."

"Prove it, and I'll get out of here and give you guys a minute alone before the wedding starts. Deal, Beginagain?"

He folded his arms. "Fine by me."

"Beginagain?" Amelia raised her eyebrows.

Bethany laughed, and while taking Amelia's BP, sang a children's song about a man named Michael Finnegan. Amelia closed her eyes and lay very still, but a smile played on her lips.

"We used to torture him with that song when he was little."

"And still do," he pointed out.

Bethany ripped the BP cuff from Amelia's arm. "You're right. Much more respectable now. I suspect once Finn and I leave, it will go down further." Bethany stood, wagging a finger. "Let's try to keep it that way, understood?" Amelia saluted.

"Don't be late," Bethy admonished as she brushed by him.

When the door closed behind her, he sank to the edge of the bed. "Alone at last."

"I'm sorry—"

"Don't apologize." He brushed Amelia's hair back from her face. "Hell, I'm flattered. You actually asked for help."

She smacked his shoulder. "Rub it in."

"Hey, watch it, you'll wrinkle the suit. Speaking of which..." He smoothed his lapels. "How do I look?"

"Fishing for compliments?"

He shrugged, both hands palm up. "If I must."

"I like you better in an apron. I'm not much of a tuxedo kind of girl. Though, I must say..."

"Yes?"

"I'd take a second look if I passed you on the street."

"Damning with faint praise. I see how it is." He stroked her forehead, then impulsively leaned down and kissed her.

She looked startled as he pulled away.

"If you need me, you know what to do."

"Oh, right. Like you'd dash from the altar."

"I would." When had she gotten under his skin? And why didn't it bother him as much as it should have? "So use your power wisely, young Jedi. I don't want to piss off my brother without good reason." Finn flashed her a slow, sexy grin as he stood.

"Hey!" she called when he'd reached the door.

He paused.

"Greg's a good guy, right? All the way through? He's not going to hurt her, right? I mean...I wouldn't want to have to stand on the balcony and object to the marriage. For one thing, your sister would be mad at me for being out of bed."

"Greg is truly one of the good guys. She dumped him once. He was a basket case. No worries that he'd do anything to hurt her, I promise. Why would you even ask?"

She shrugged. "Just...wondered, that's all. I like Shannon. Now go, before you're late and they send a search party after you."

Her concern for Shannon touched him. Jordan wasn't outside the room, so he clattered down the back staircase. He pulled up short at the lower landing. For a long moment he stared at the empty wall.

At the space where his and Amelia's wedding picture hung in the dream.

He shook his head. "Nah." Two strikes and he was out of that game.

And yet...the image stayed in his head while Greg and Shannon exchanged their vows.

After their photographer snapped a seemingly never-ending series of shots, he went upstairs to check on Amelia before they left for the Erie Club and the reception. Finn used to be a chef there before opening Fresh.

She was sound asleep.

As long as he dared, he stood and watched, listened to her even breathing. His fingers itched to touch her. He found a wedding invitation one of his sisters had left on the dresser, and a pen. Folding the heavy paper in half he scrawled a note on the back and stood it on the bedside table.

Wish you were there....

"Jordan! Jordan, come here!" Uncle Greg waved at her from the archway that led into the banquet room. His voice barely carried over the music from the DJ. "There's someone I want you to meet."

"Okay!" She turned from the dance floor, where people were slapping their elbows in the chicken dance, and shut her video camera. Minutes earlier she'd taped Uncle Hayden and Aunt Judy doing a rumba almost worthy of a *Dancing with the Stars* episode. She'd had no idea he could dance like that.

She'd been glad she hadn't known how good he was when she'd danced with him, and stepped on his toes five or six times.

Jordan scurried over to Uncle Greg, who'd peeled his jacket off and rolled up his sleeves. Beside him stood... She forced herself to walk more slowly. More ladylike.

"Jordan, this is Ty." Uncle Greg gestured to the teenage boy who stood at his side. "Ty had a bone marrow transplant...what's it been? About a year and a half now?"

"Yeah, something like that." Ty had wavy brown hair and hazel eyes that sparkled as he gave her a slow once-over. Her heart pounded.

"I thought maybe you'd like to talk to him. To ask questions about the procedure. You don't mind, do you, Ty? This is my niece Jordan, the one I've been telling you about."

"Sure, no problem."

Jordan wanted to squeal. Instead, she offered her hand. "Nice to meet you."

He enfolded her fingers in his grip. Butterflies rumbaed in her stomach.

"Nice to meet you, too."

Across the room, someone clanged silverware against glass. The ringing spread quickly until the sound overpowered the music.

Uncle Greg's face reddened and he scanned the dance

floor. "Better find my bride, or they'll never stop. You kids have fun." He waded into the thick of the crowd, which parted for him. Aunt Shannon, gorgeous in her short white dress, met him in the middle of the floor and they kissed, causing the clanking to stop and everyone to clap.

"It's kind of loud in here. Let's go someplace quieter."

"Okay." Jordan followed him out of the ballroom and down the hallway. Massive stairs split, one set leading up, the other down.

"Here," Ty said, dropping to the bottom step of the stairs leading to the third floor, his back against the wall. Jordan sat beside him, her back to the banister.

"So, what do you want to know?"

Jordan shrugged. "Why did you need a BMT?"

"Leukemia."

"Oh. My uncle Ian died from leukemia." The night of the ballgame Finn had told her, in great detail, the story of his brother.

"Sorry."

Jordan covered her mouth. "Oh, no, I'm sorry. Maybe I shouldn't have said that. He didn't actually die from the leukemia. He got pneumonia before he could get his bone marrow transplant, and died."

Ty loosened his necktie. "Happens."

"Did your hair fall out? You have beautiful hair." Hesitantly, Jordan reached out to touch it.

His cheeks flushed. "Yeah. It had only just started growing back again, too, from the chemo I'd had weeks earlier. But the chemo before the transplant can be rough. You'll puke. And your hair will fall out." He pulled on one of her curls. It bounced up when he let go. "But as you can see...it grows back."

Jordan sighed. "I was hoping it wouldn't happen. I don't want to be bald."

"Like I said, it grows back." He pulled a cell phone out of his back pocket. "You wanna see a picture of me bald?"

Jordan nodded, leaning closer to look at the screen. "Oh. See, boys can get away with it. You're cute even without hair." Her face scorched.

He smiled at her, and her stomach quivered again. "Cute, huh?"

She glanced down at her lap. "Yeah."

"You're not so bad yourself. How old are you?"

Jordan's mind raced. What was the right answer? "How old do you think I am?"

"Fifteen?"

She smiled. "Good guess. How old are you?"

"Sixteen." He fingered her curl again. "What else you want to know?"

They talked for a while about being sick, missing school, and friends staying away because they were afraid. Eventually Ty produced his cell phone. She plugged the earbud he offered into her ear, while he took the other. A few minutes later, he took her hand, pulled her to her feet. With a smile that made her heart start to pound, he led her to the landing at the top of the stairs. After a furtive glance around, he walked her backward until she bumped into the wall. "You're really pretty," he whispered.

Her legs trembled, and a rush of heat made her think she was in Fresh's kitchen in the midst of dinner service. The thudding of her heart made the music hard to hear.

He lowered his head...she closed her eyes.

His lips brushed over hers. *Soft.*

She prayed she wouldn't make a fool of herself. Then she kissed him back. Her hands fluttered at her sides, then she lifted them, settling them around his shoulders.

He slipped his around her waist, pulling her closer.

With her pulse double-timing, she followed his lead, parting her lips, letting the tip of her tongue connect with his.

Abruptly he jerked away from her, pulling the earbud out of her ear.

"Hey, Casanova, what the hell do you think you're doing?"

Jordan opened her eyes to find Uncle Hayden with his hand clamped on Ty's shoulder. The spare earbud dangled by the wire. Ty sputtered.

Hayden leaned closer, peering at her. "Your nose is bleeding. Damn it. Boy, I'm going to count to one, and you'd better be gone. One." If looks could kill, Ty would have dropped dead on the spot. Great.

Ty barreled for the stairs, sending an apologetic glance over his shoulder when he was halfway down and well out of Hayden's reach. Jordan touched her nose. When she pulled her hand away, blood dripped from her fingertips.

Uncle Hayden fished in his jacket for a handkerchief. "Here. Use this."

Jordan held it over her nostrils, pinching them shut. She tipped her head back, ignoring the metallic taste of blood running down her throat.

"Sweetheart, are you okay?"

"I was *fine* until you got here."

"You're *bleeding*."

She lifted one shoulder. "I get nosebleeds sometimes. It wasn't his fault."

"Don't you know better than to go off alone with a guy?"

She sighed contentedly. "I got my first kiss. It was wonderful. And scary. At the same time. Haven't you ever felt that way?"

Uncle Hayden raked his hand through his short hair, spiking the longer strands in the front. "Yeah, I'm familiar with the sensation. Watch yourself, kid. It's highly addictive."

"Are you going to tell?"

"I haven't decided yet." He guided her to a chair and eased her down in it. Then he took the handkerchief, keeping pressure on her nose for several minutes. "Let's see if this has stopped." He gingerly let go.

Blood flooded out, all over the white skirt of her dress. "Oh!"

He clamped the cloth over her nose again, pinching it shut with one hand and pushing her head forward so the excess missed her clothes, spattering onto the floor. "Keep your head level. And don't sweat the dress." He dug out his cell phone with his free hand, stabbing buttons with his thumb. "Elke? I'm on the landing at the top of the stairs by the bathrooms. I've got a big problem. Jordan's got a nosebleed. A gusher. I can't get it to stop. No, I don't have her head back. I know better than that. Okay, we'll meet you downstairs. Thanks." He slipped his phone back into his pocket.

"Looks like we're going to the hospital, pip," he said.

Still on a high—Shelby was so not going to believe this!—Jordan smiled up at him and shrugged again. "Even if every last drop dripped out, it was worth it."

Uncle Hayden shook his head. "No need to get all Juliet about it. It was just a kiss. There'll be plenty more of those in your future."

"As long as I have one." She gagged and coughed, spraying his tuxedo with blood.

His eyes widened. He bent down, scooping her up with one strong arm as if she were a ventriloquist doll, keeping the other hand firmly clamped on her nose. "Don't talk like that. Hasn't working with Greg taught you anything about positive thinking?"

She tried to nod. "Positive. More kisses in the future."

"Stop talking!" Hayden blew out a long breath as he raced her down the stairs. "No question. I'm definitely telling your father."

CHAPTER TWELVE

HAYDEN PUNCHED IN the code, then held the door as Finn carried Jordan's sleeping form up the last steps.

"Thanks," Finn murmured. "For everything." Hayden had ditched the woman he'd been flirting with—someone he and Greg knew from the Children's Cancer Center, apparently—and insisted Elke stay behind to enjoy the reception. He'd gone to the hospital with them. His presence had allowed Finn the opportunity to slip outside the hospital and call Amelia from time to time.

The doctor had packed Jordan's nose with gauze and given her a transfusion and platelets. Because of the packing and her condition, she'd also be taking antibiotics as a precaution.

Hayden rolled a shoulder. "Always got your back, man."

"As long as it doesn't involve a secret, yeah."

His brother grinned, offering a middle finger, then disappeared into his room. Finn carted Jordan down the hall.

"Finn?" Amelia called. "Is that you? How's Jordan?"

"Basically knocked out." He stopped outside their bedrooms. "Let me get her settled and—"

"No! I need to see her. Bring her in here, please?"

He nudged the door open with his foot and laid Jordan on the near side of the bed.

Amelia rolled onto her side to face her daughter. She stroked her forehead, then fingered the sleeve of the yellow hospital pajamas. "Where's her dress?"

"In a bag in the foyer. It's probably unsalvageable. It's covered in blood."

"So's your tux."

He glanced down. The jacket was still in the backseat of his Explorer. The white shirt looked like he'd lost an ax fight. "Yeah, I'm thinking Hayden and I aren't getting our deposits back."

"Sorry."

He shrugged. "Not like it's your fault." He crossed to his dresser and rummaged in a drawer. Only some of his clothes had moved with him into the other room. He peeled off the bloody shirt, dropped a T-shirt over his head.

"Someday you have to tell me about that tat."

Glancing over his shoulder, he found Amelia watching him. He kept the shirt bunched around his neck. "What, this?" The blue-eyed white tiger had been another of his impulsive decisions, though one that had lasted longer than both his marriages put together. Some days you just had to say "what the hell" and go with it. Mistakes were easier to live with than regrets. That was the lesson he'd learned from Ian...one he'd been forgetting lately. Too busy worrying about failing. Failing at his business, failing at his life.

"You got another one?"

He fished an old pair of jeans out of the bottom dresser drawer. "I do. Maybe someday I'll show you."

Being that the four crossed swords graced his left butt cheek—a location specifically chosen so his mother wouldn't see it, or the matching tats on Greg's and Hayden's rears—they'd have to be on rather intimate terms.

He popped into the bathroom, exchanging black tuxedo pants for the jeans, then peeling off the black dress socks. Barefooted and much more comfortable, he padded back to where Jordan lay.

"Why is she so out of it?" Amelia caressed the girl's face.

"Diphenhydramine. She had a mild allergic reaction after the transfusion."

Amelia's head jerked up. "What? Why didn't you tell me?"

"I'm telling you now. Like I said, it was mild. Best guess the docs have is that the donor ate a bunch of tomatoes before donating, and Jordan's body reacted like it does when she eats too many herself. She got a rash. I had no idea that could happen."

"Oh, sweetie. As if you haven't had enough problems. My poor baby."

A goofy grin tugged at Jordan's mouth. Her eyelids fluttered opened, and she stared blearily at Amelia. "Mommy?"

"Yes, baby, I'm here now."

The grin widened. "Ty kissed me, Mommy."

Amelia exchanged a bemused look with Finn. "So I heard."

Jordan sighed. "It was wonderful. And scary. And...wonderful." Her eyes shuttered again, and her head lolled to the side.

"Her first kiss, and I wasn't there for her to share about it with me."

Finn snorted, perching on the edge of the bed. "I doubt most kids share about their first kiss with their mothers. If not for Hayden catching them in the act, we'd have never known about it."

"Don't be so sure. We have a very close relationship."

He swung his legs onto the bed, stretching out on his side, sandwiching Jordan between them. "We could poll my sisters. I doubt any of them told our mom, and they're all pretty tight."

"Jordan *told* me." Amelia's mouth set in a firm line.

"She's drugged. Did you see her face? She looked like she'd spent hours standing downwind of a Grateful Dead concert."

When Amelia's lower lip started to quiver, he back-pedaled. "Hey, now. I was just teasing you." He reached across Jordan to brush his fingers across Amelia's cheek. "She did tell you. You guys have a terrific relationship. As to missing out on a first..." He moved his hand to his daughter's face. "I missed them all. Kind of nice that I got to hear about this one before you did."

Amelia stared at him for a moment. "You weren't entitled to them," she said gently.

"I know." But now... Things had changed for him tonight. At the idea of missing the rest of her life, of missing all of Chip's firsts, a big hole opened in the middle of Finn's chest. He stroked Jordan's forehead.

"I didn't mean for you to get hurt in this," Amelia murmured.

Gruffly, he cleared his throat. "I know that, too." He slipped one arm behind Jordan's neck, the other under her knees. "I'm going to put her to bed now."

Amelia pressed a quick kiss to their daughter's forehead before Finn lifted her.

After settling her in, he returned to Amelia's room, standing in the doorway. "Anything else you need?"

"Company?" She patted the covers next to her. His pained

expression when he'd left...she needed to know what was going on in his head. Where he...where *she*...stood.

"I dunno. Wasn't it too much company that made your blood pressure shoot up today?"

"That was forever ago. I've been all alone since then. Besides, I'm used to you. You don't make my blood pressure shoot up."

"Way to bolster my ego," he muttered. "You don't mind if I lie down, do you?"

He exhaled loudly as he lowered himself to his side, then propped his head in his palm. "After taking her to the doctor's a few times, I thought I knew how all this worked. Thought I could stay detached. But I have never felt terror like I did when Hayden brought her into the ballroom and I saw all that blood. I swear, I aged ten years in ten seconds."

"Scary, isn't it?" The terror in his voice when he'd called to tell her about the situation had touched Amelia. Deeply.

"Yeah." His eyes shimmered. He lowered his head.

"Hey..." She threaded her fingers into his dark hair, pulled his head to her shoulder.

Stiff and unyielding at first, he eventually sighed, relaxing into her. She stroked the silky waves. Damp warmth spread into her nightshirt near her collarbone. "Are you crying?" she murmured. She wanted to wrap her arms around him, assure him everything would be all right—just like she did for Jordan. "Hell, no."

"Either tears or blood are seeping into my nightshirt from your face, and we've had enough blood for one day."

"Amen to that." The gentle whoosh of the central air filled the silence. "It was bad. Made me realize exactly how many things can go wrong for her. Bleeding, infection..."

"Ahhh. You were thinking about your brother, and what happened to him. And applying that to Jordan." Amelia's heart clenched. For the first time, she had someone who shared her darkest fear.

His shoulder twitched against her body. He lifted his head. Tear tracks stained his cheeks. He brusquely dragged the back of his hand over his face, wiping them away. "I...I can't lose her, Amelia. Not to an infection, not to the aplastic anemia... Not to you. I might not have been entitled to it in the past. But tonight changed everything. Tonight, I became a dad, Amelia. Not a sperm donor. She's my daughter. And I'm claiming her."

Stunned, Amelia stared at him.

He draped his palm over her belly. "Chip, too. A son needs a father. I want to be part of their lives."

He framed her face with his hands, pressed his lips to hers. "Part of yours," he whispered.

"Did you save the best for last, or am I an afterthought?"

He took her mouth again, harder. Driven. Desperate.

She matched him for intensity, demanding more. Letting their emotions swirl around them like a tempest. Finally pulling away from her, he growled, "Did that feel like you're an afterthought? Or how about this?" He shifted, pressing a rock-hard erection against her hip.

Heart hammering, and with her brain still off-line from his kiss, she shook her head.

His megawatt sexy grin slid into place.

"W-what?"

"Your hair is rumpled, your eyes are languid and your face is flushed. There's something extremely satisfying in knowing

I made you look that way."

"Arrogant, arrogant man." She cupped him through the denim, smug at his sharp intake of breath and the way his body bucked in response. "And who made you like this? Hmm...I think that would be me."

"Evil woman." He hissed as she rubbed him, then reached down and clamped her wrist, stilling her. "Don't stoke a fire we can't put out, Amelia. It's cruel and unusual punishment."

"Tell me about it." Despite his grip, she managed to wiggle her fingers, making him twitch again. "I can put this fire out. I've been thinking about it a lot. Let me touch you, Finn. Let me...make you feel good."

He groaned. "Don't tempt me. But I'm not about to engage in...fun...when you can't have some, too. It's not fair."

"Fair? What part of any of this is fair, Finn? Didn't you tell Chip the day of the surgery that life's not fair, and he should learn that now? I mean, our daughter's facing a life-threatening disease and—"

"What did you say?"

"Huh? Life's not fair?"

He shook his head, then flopped onto his back. "Our daughter. You called her *our* daughter."

The urge to deny it burned her tongue. But after all he'd done, after his tears, his obvious love for Jordan..."Yeah. I guess I did."

He sighed. "Wow."

"A pronoun doesn't mean all that much. I can give you a pronoun after tonight."

"Gee, thanks."

He returned to his side, looking down at her. "What exactly is the plan, Amelia? For after, I mean. Does that pronoun come with any actual benefits later on, or is it just an empty word?"

She shrugged. "You...this whole situation...my plans are blown to hell. Right now, believe it or not, I'm just trying to get through one day at a time."

"One day at a time. Okay. That will work for now, I suppose. But not forever, Amelia. I want more."

Her stomach tightened. She wanted more, too, but wasn't sure what more looked like. She did know what it *didn't* look like—it didn't look like marriage.

Spending time together in her bed became something of a habit. One Amelia found she really enjoyed. They talked, they snuggled, they kissed...sometimes they simply lay there in companionable silence.

Other times they lay there in seething hot, frustrated silence, struggling with desire they couldn't quench. Exasperating as hell to have a batteries-not-required partner but not be able to make use of him. And the stubborn man continued to refuse to allow her to alleviate *his* frustration.

For four long weeks.

The stubborn man in question glanced over at her from the driver's seat of his Explorer. They'd stopped, she assumed at some sort of intersection. Hard to see the landscape when you were completely reclined in the passenger seat.

"How you feeling over there?"

Amelia tightened her grip on the shoulder portion of the seat belt. The lap portion rode well below her rounded tummy. "Good. Relieved. I mean, at least we know Chip is now sort of out of the woods."

Late that Sunday afternoon, out of consideration for Amelia so she didn't have to run into other patients, Bethany had administered an ultrasound in her office. At thirty-five weeks along, Chip was pronounced fully viable. They'd rushed the development of his lungs with steroid injections so that if he was born now, he'd be fine.

Still small, but able to breathe.

But for them, for *Jordan,* size mattered. So they had to hope he didn't come early. The stitches that secured him in the womb would stay put until week thirty-eight or thirty-nine, unless Amelia began experiencing contractions, or an increased sense of pressure. In which case Bethany would remove them immediately.

Finally, they were in the home stretch. Although five more weeks in bed until she hit full-term did seem like another eternity. She'd written three journal articles, revamped the office bookkeeping system, to Sia's dismay, and built a new Web site for the office. She was running out of actual productive things to do. She sighed. "I wish we didn't have to go straight back to the house. Just driving around, even though I can't see a damn thing, is such a treat."

"You're in luck then," Finn said, as the car began to move again, "'cause I have a surprise for you."

Amelia's stomach churned and she shivered—a Pavlovian response to the word. "You know I hate surprises."

"You'd rather go back to bed now?"

She gritted her teeth. This was Finn. Not Ron or whatever his real name was. "Are those my only two choices?"

"Yep."

She rode in silence.

He chuckled. "You're actually thinking about it, aren't you? Come on, be brave. Face the big, bad surprise. I think you'll like it. I've put a lot of effort into it."

A lot of effort? "You're not helping." Still...going back to staring at the ceiling in his room... "Okay. I'll take the surprise."

"That's my girl."

His girl. The concept didn't jar as much as she expected. In fact, she sort of liked the idea. The last few weeks, drawing closer to him, she'd realized that maybe she had been shortchanging herself. Her daughter.

The gentle motion of the car, combined with actually being out of the bed, being pregnant, and the relief over Chip, made her snooze. She started awake each time they stopped.

Finally, he parked. "We're here. Give me a few moments to take care of some stuff, okay?"

"Okay."

The car rocked as he shut his door. The tailgate opened, and she tried to catch a glimpse of what he was doing. To no avail. She couldn't see a damn thing. And she couldn't sit up without his help.

He made two more trips to the car before he opened her door and offered her his arm. Finally upright, she glanced out the windshield while the wave of dizziness passed.

A weathered picnic table sat in the sand only yards beyond the car, near the gently lapping lake. Alongside it, he'd pitched a beach umbrella. He'd staked a red-and-white checked cloth to the sand, beside it, an air mattress.

"Oh..." Amelia eased herself out of the car.

Finn scooped her into his arms, trudging through the sand. He carefully sank to his knees, then settled her on the mattress. He peeled off her slippers. "Gotta have bare feet at the beach." He smiled at her. "I have a few more things to get. You good?"

She nodded. "I'm so good I could burst."

"No bursting. That would be messy. Good surprise, right?"

It certainly beat being left at the airport while your bank accounts were cleaned out. "Right."

He jumped up and headed back to the Explorer.

Amelia smoothed the denim circus tent she wore, tucking the edges under her to keep it from blowing. Fashion, never her strongest suit anyway, had been another casualty of her situation.

The wind fanned her skin. The low-riding sun warmed her feet. She wiggled her toes and sighed.

Finn returned with a wicker picnic basket and a silver bucket with a bottle sticking out of it. "Sparkling grape juice," he explained.

"This...this is amazing, Finn. Is this the same spot where you made the video with Jordan?"

"You're getting ahead of me." He scooted across the picnic blanket to her. With a hesitant smile, he uncurled his hand.

Glad you're here.

She lifted his ink-covered palm to her mouth, pressed a kiss to it. "I'm glad, too."

Instead of the fried chicken he'd prepared for their indoor beach picnic, this time he'd pulled out all the stops. Shrimp. Bite-size pieces of filet mignon. A medley of summer squash roasted in olive oil. A potato chip and marshmallow fluff sandwich on white bread that they shared, him grimacing, her laughing. The elegant flute he used to serve her sparkling grape juice made her laugh more. "Somehow the straw detracts from the crystal more than the lack of alcohol does, don't you think?"

He shrugged. "We do the best we can with what we have. Or what we need. Or something like that." He clinked his glass against hers. "To making lemon meringue pie when life gives us lemons."

"You're not calling me a lemon, are you?" She took a sip from the straw.

His blue eyes twinkled. "No. But now that you mention it..."

A man and woman strolling the beach slowed as they passed. "Aww," the woman said. "How romantic."

Face flushing, Finn saluted her with his champagne flute.

As the couple walked farther down the beach, the woman whacked the man on the shoulder with the shoes she was holding. "Jerk." The wind carried her complaint to them. "How come you don't do something romantic like that for me?"

"Ow." The man rubbed his arm. "We're at the beach enjoying the sunset. Take it or leave it."

Amelia bit her lip, but burst into laughter once the couple were out of sight. Finn laughed, too.

"Poor guy," she said, once her giggles had died down. "You set the bar too high for him to follow."

"Because you're worth it." Finn leaned over to kiss her. Suitable for public viewing, it was sweet. Tender.

She completely melted.

He cleaned up their dinner mess, repacking the basket. Then he stretched out beside her. The wispy clouds over the lake turned cotton candy pink. Then peach. Then orange.

Finn fidgeted.

Finally, she turned her head from the glorious setting sun to him. "You're wiggling like a five-year-old on too much sugar. Do you have sand fleas in your pants or what?"

"Um...or what." He rose to his knees on the picnic blanket, fumbling in his pocket. "Amelia, I know I've already got two strikes against me, but I'm thinking the third time's the charm. I don't want to lose you. Or the kids."

Amelia's heart began to pound. *No, dear God, please, don't let him go where I think he's going.*

"I know it's not what either of us planned, but I want us to be together. A real family."

Her stomach tightened.

The little box creaked as he snapped it open. Sunlight caught in the diamond, casting tiny rainbows across her. "Amelia, will you marry me?"

She covered her mouth with a trembling hand. Her pulse thundered in her ears. "Oh...Finn. Oh, God." She shook her head as the lovely dinner he'd fed her churned in her stomach. "Marriage...I—I...no. I don't do marriage."

His eyes widened. Then his brows drew together. "But—"

"No. No, no, no." Her whole body shook. Marriage? Because of the kids? To be a family?

"Take some time, Amelia...."

The first man had taken her money. Her pride.

This one wanted something even more precious.

Her children.

Bile rose in her throat. She rolled in the opposite direction of him, coming to rest on her hands and knees on the sand.

He held back her hair while she lost her dinner.

CHAPTER THIRTEEN

EVEN HIS HAIR HURT.

Finn stared morosely at the five shot glasses he'd lined up on the kitchen island's serving bar, alongside the almost full bottle of vodka with a pouring spout.

He'd expected some hesitation from her. But not an outright no. And definitely not an *oh, hell, no.*

She'd gutted him with a teaspoon, and he was doing his best to deal with it. He'd knocked back two of the shots before midnight, just to take the edge off, but was waiting to do some serious damage until...

A key turned in the back door, and Hayden sauntered in from his late-night date. He'd postponed his own plans and taken Jordan to the movies earlier, knowing only that Finn had planned a special dinner for Amelia and wanted Jordan occupied.

Finn hadn't said a word to Amelia since the beach, simply brought her home and returned her to bed. He'd done his damnedest to act normal when Jordan came home. Now both of them were asleep upstairs.

And he'd spend the night back in his temporary room.

Alone.

"Good. You're home." He tossed another shot down his throat.

"Didn't know I had a curfew, Dad."

"No curfew. I just want someone else here in case Amelia or Jordan need anything. I'm about to get shit-faced."

Hayden dropped onto the second stool, glancing over the bar. "So I see. What's the occasion?"

Finn fumbled in his pocket, then slapped the ring box on the island counter. He reached for shot number four.

"It's not legal in this state for us to get married, bro, but I appreciate the kind offer."

Finn snorted, then winced, eyes watering as the vodka burned his nasal passages. He lifted the next glass, raised it in Hayden's direction. "That's a nicer rejection than I got from Amelia. *Salud!*" He fired back the liquor.

"What? Here I thought you were looking for courage. You already asked, and she said no?"

"Not only did she say no multiple times, she threw up. She's taking freakin' antinausea meds, but the idea of marrying me was that appalling." That moment was seared into his memory. His divorces had hurt far less. He lifted the bottle, refilled the line of glasses.

"Harsh. Yeah, that calls for some alcohol-induced amnesia." Hayden culled three glasses from the line. "Still...let's not get carried away, huh?" He went to the racks of clean dishes by the commercial dishwasher, pulled out two water glasses and added ice. Returning to the island, he dumped Finn's two shots into one, and three into the other, which he kept for himself. "Let's move to sipping rather than shooting."

"Hey, I'm taking it like a man."

Hayden laughed. "Real men don't risk alcohol poisoning, so slow it down."

"Who'da thunk it? You, the voice of reason when it comes

to women. I didn't intend to become a real dad. But it happened." Finn laid his head on his arm.

"Do you love her?"

"Yeah."

"What makes you so sure it's love? And why on earth does that mean you have to marry her?"

"Greg said it the day of his wedding. I won't risk losing her. Them. I started thinking about what happens when Chip's born. She's so damn independent, which is good. And bad. She'll be gone before I can even think. And I couldn't imagine my life without them. How empty it would be. That's love, right? When you can't imagine life without someone?" He barked a wry laugh.

"Imagine life without them... Hmm..." Hayden took another drink. "I think that's the answer right there."

Finn raised his head, then blinked hard to focus on his brother's face. "What?"

"Remember when Shannon dumped Greg last year? How he kept wanting to run over to her apartment? And what did we both tell him?"

"Give her space. Let her come to her senses."

"Exactly. And that's what you need to do. You gotta give her a chance to miss you. Before she gets the green light to split."

Finn snorted. "How the hell am I supposed to do that?" He gestured at the ceiling. "She's sleeping up there! She's dependent on me for almost everything right now."

"Set her free. Let her depend on someone else. Give her space."

He stared at his brother.

Hayden took the glass from his hand, set it on the counter. "Send her to Mom and Dad's."

###

Amelia blinked back the tears burning her eyes. Dressed for the second day in a row, which should have made it a special occasion, she lay on top of the comforter, not feeling very comforted.

She refused to cry. Especially where Jordan could see.

Her daughter folded her arms across her chest and stomped a sandal-clad foot. "I'm not going. I'm staying here."

"You'll do as you're told, Jordan." The weariness of her voice wouldn't convince anyone, let alone a teenager, that she had the energy to enforce her command.

"No. I won't. You still haven't told me why we have to go. I'm not stupid. I know you had a fight about something. What happened last night?"

Hayden appeared in the doorway, shifting from foot to foot. He'd been charged with loading their stuff into Finn's Explorer and moving them.

"Ask your fath—Finn." He was putting her out. He hadn't given her a chance to explain how she cared for him, was sorry she'd hurt him... Hell, she'd crushed him; she'd seen it in his eyes. But marrying wasn't something she'd ever do again. Ever.

"I did. He said to ask you."

"What can I tell you?" Amelia shrugged.

"The truth!"

"I'll tell you, pip." Hayden glared at Amelia. "Finn asked your mother to marry him and make him part of your family for good. She said no, and broke his heart. Having her around now would hurt him too much, so you're moving to Grandma and Grandpa's. End of story."

Jordan's arms dropped to her sides, and her mouth gaped open. "He asked...you said *no?* I can't believe it." She left abruptly, pounding down the back staircase.

"Hayden! What the hell do you think you're doing?"

"Letting the cat out of the bag. It's not good to keep cats in bags. Things die that way."

"It wasn't your place."

"Ask me if I care." He stalked to the bed and scooped Amelia into his arms. Though anger radiated from him, he held her gently as he started from the room.

"Wait, wait! I'm not ready." She grabbed on to the door frame as he was carrying her through.

"The longer you wait, the harder it's going to be." Compassion softened his tone. "Just let go."

Sage advice. No point in trying to hang on to a man she never intended to marry. One who'd shown that when things didn't go his way, he'd kick her out on her ass.

Just like her stepfathers—and some of the "uncles"—had done to her mother.

Swallowing hard, Amelia slowly released her death grip on the wooden frame. She looped her arms around his neck. Hayden headed down the hall.

"Aren't we using the back stairs?"

"No. He's in the kitchen, prepping for lunch. He's already bandaged three fingers this morning, and I'd rather he didn't actually slice one off."

Her throat constricted. She struggled to speak. "What

about Jordan?"

"Maybe it would be best if we get you settled first. I can come back for Jordan later. I'll bring your car over, too."

Leave her daughter, who was now mad at her, with Finn, who was equally mad? That didn't sound like much of a plan. Still, it would give her a chance to figure out what to say to Jordan.

In the foyer, Hayden set her on her feet. She walked through the two sets of double doors onto the porch. Memories, images, of her first meeting with Finn in this very spot assailed her.

He'd worn unbuttoned jeans and a smug smile, and she'd fallen in lust at first sight. He'd been sperm donor #7364, contributor of the other set of chromosomes that had created her daughter's DNA.

Now...he really was Jordan's father. Lust had turned into something deeper. And just as she'd feared, hearts were breaking all over the place. Including hers.

He'd actually made her start to believe that maybe, just maybe, he was different. A prince in toad clothing instead of the other way around. Marriage wasn't possible, but couldn't they have had some kind of relationship without it?

She didn't doubt that he loved Jordan. But he'd had trouble dealing with the medical realities of her condition.

If the transplant didn't work...how would he cope?

The stats regarding parents of extremely ill children and the dissolution of their relationships were even higher than the norm. And ninety-nine times out of a hundred, it was the man who walked when things got rough.

They had enough on their plates without adding that to it.

Hayden swept Amelia's legs out from under her, hefting her in his arms again and descending to the sidewalk. She turned her head to stare at the building as he carried her to the parking lot.

"I didn't want to hurt him when I showed up on his doorstep. I just wanted to save my daughter's life."

"Despite the pain, I think it's safe to say my brother wouldn't change that. Wouldn't change Jordan showing up on his doorstep, either." Hayden opened the door to Finn's Explorer.

Amelia let him lift her to the seat, which she reclined slowly. Fresh and its surroundings disappeared from her sight line. She buckled her seat belt, then blinked back a new surge of tears as he backed out the car. "There were no other options."

Hayden snorted. "Right. Keep telling yourself that if it makes you feel better."

"Your brother has two failed marriages under his belt already. What possessed him to *propose* to me?"

"Men in love do stupid things."

"Love? You really think he's in love with me? He never mentioned love." Even if he had, love was easy to claim. Easy to fake, too.

"What I think doesn't matter. I'm not the one proposing to you."

"And you think proposing to me was stupid?"

Hayden shrugged, keeping his eyes on the road. "Look what it got him."

Amelia sighed. "Everything was going great. Why'd he have to ruin it?"

"Because he's terrified that after Chip's born, you'll take him and Jordan back to Maine. And Finn will miss out on his kids' lives."

A chill raised goose bumps on her arms. "That's what I thought."

"What?"

"This is about my children, not me." Amelia laid a hand over her belly. Her son stirred beneath her palm.

"Believe that if you want, but Finn wants it all. The whole package. That includes you. You've got to admit it seems like fate's at work here, no?"

"We make our own fate."

Finn might have been willing to risk a third go-round with marriage, but once had been more than enough for her.

Jordan slumped against the island's serving counter. Not even the scent of the cooling triple chocolate brownies could cheer her up.

How could it when they might be the last batch she ever made with her father? Why were adults so stupid?

Pans clattered against the stovetop as he seared tuna for one of the lunch customers and tossed some veggies with olive oil in another. "Can Grandma cook?"

He glanced over his shoulder at her, smiling. "Yes, Grandma can cook. You've been to Sunday dinner."

"Yeah, and you've brought a lot of food to it."

Her cell phone chattered on the counter. She grabbed it. A text from Shelby, who was back in Maine to start school in a week. Jordan was enrolled in a cyberschool until she was cleared to go back after her transplant. Aunt Kara had promised to help her, too.

Got ur voice mail. Whazzup? Shelby's message read.

My parents r fighting. Like getting divorced w/o even getting married 1st, Jordan fired back.

WTH? Thought it all good? What happened?

F asked M 2 marry him. She said NO! =:-o

Ur mom is nutz. I'd marry him.

Shut up. This is serious. What should I do?

Sorry. :(Not much u can do. Does this mean ur coming home sooner?

No. Still can't cause of Chip. Moving to G&G's house.

The back door opened, and Uncle Hayden trudged in. Their eyes met and he pressed his lips together, then crooked his finger.

Crap! Gotta go. TTYL. She slipped her phone into her pocket. Pretending she hadn't noticed her uncle, she turned to watch her father work. He moved like a dancer in the kitchen, stirring, flipping, sliding things in and out of the ovens. She picked up her video camera and turned it on.

Uncle Hayden appeared in the frame. He leaned close to Finn, spoke so low she couldn't hear what he said.

Her dad nodded.

Jordan's throat closed, and the viewfinder got blurry.

Finn spun from the stove to the island, plating the dishes. He squirted sauces, arranged things precisely, then wiped the edges of the plates. As soon as he set them on the far end of the serving counter, Tracey, one of the waitresses, appeared through the swinging doors as though summoned by his thoughts. When she left, he looked up at her.

"Time to go, Jordan."

She shut the camera, her bottom lip quivering. Tears started to run down her cheeks.

"Oh, hey, don't do that." He came around the island to where she perched on the stool. His own eyes shimmered suspiciously.

She wrapped her arms around his waist, pressed her face into his chest. He stroked her hair. "There's no crying in the kitchen," he said gently.

"I don't want to go," she choked out. "I want to stay with you."

"I don't want you to go, either." He reached down, easing her away and lifting her chin, forcing her to look at him. "But I need you to take care of your mom."

"She—she can take care of herself. She always has."

"She can't right now. She needs you."

Jordan shook her head. "She needs *you*. *I* need you, Dad."

His eyes widened. "Oh, sweetheart..." He stroked his thumb over her cheek, wiping away her tears. "Your mom made it very clear that I'm not the person she needs, or wants, in her life."

"You love her?"

His Adam's apple bobbed as he swallowed. He nodded. "I do."

"Why?"

"Why? Because she's smart and funny. She's independent and strong. She takes excellent care of you. She makes a plan, then makes it happen." He shrugged. "Your mom's an amazing woman."

"And me? Do you love me?"

He pulled her tight against him, squeezing her. "With all my heart. Don't you ever doubt that."

Sobs shook her. She finally had a father, one who loved her. Had a real family, with aunts and uncles and cousins.

And she had to give it up.

"Hey, if not for your baby brother acting up, we wouldn't have had this much time. Let's be thankful for what we've had, right?"

"No. I don't want to be thankful for what I've had. I want more." Of everything. More love. More family. More life.

"So do I, sweetie. So do I."

Amelia stared up at the new ceiling. A popcorn ceiling. And while only a day ago a change of scenery had been most welcome, the popcorn ceiling with its thousands of little dots just annoyed her.

The twin bed pushed against the faded pink wall hemmed her in far more than Finn's queen-size bed. A single night table between the two twin beds left little room for all her junk, and she missed his hundred channels of nothing to watch.

The two high rectangular windows were positioned over her head, leaving her with only the room to stare at. For all she knew, the world no longer existed outside this space.

Lydia Hawkins, Finn's mother, appeared in the doorway. Amelia could only hope to look as good when she was Lydia's age. Silver hair framed a face enhanced by well-earned wrinkles, around blue eyes that she'd passed to her children and grandchildren.

Blue eyes that nearly froze Amelia with their icy disdain.

She got the idea Lydia wasn't entirely thrilled with her new houseguest. But then, if anyone hurt Jordan, Amelia wouldn't be thrilled with having to care for them, either.

"Here's your mother, dear. We weren't sure if you'd want to stay right in here with her. There's another twin bed."

Jordan, at Lydia's shoulder, scowled. "Is there someplace else I can stay?"

"Absolutely. You can have the bedroom that shares a bathroom with this one." Lydia slid open the pocket door that led to the Jack-and-Jill bathroom. Jordan, backpack slung over one shoulder, followed her.

"There are two straps on that backpack for a reason," Amelia called after her.

"Whatever, Mom."

Well, at least her daughter was still speaking to her.

The afternoon wore on. Lydia brought her a dinner tray with meat loaf, mashed potatoes and carrots. All extremely hard to eat while lying down. And though the food was tasty enough, it wasn't Finn's carefully prepared feasts. No frog carved from a green pepper staring up at her, no cauliflower-and-black-olive sheep grazing on her veggies.

She dozed after dinner, then updated her Facebook page, played another word in her Scrabble game with Sia, and surfed the net. Like an addict seeking a fix, she even tried to access Finn's kitchen cam, with no luck. Around ten, she heard Jordan in the bathroom, brushing her teeth. "Jordan?"

Her daughter popped her head through the doorway, toothbrush sticking out of her mouth. "Yeah?"

"Come say good-night when you're done."

She grunted, then disappeared back into the bathroom.

A few minutes later, she once again stood in the opening of the pocket door. "Good night." She turned away.

"Hey! That's it? Come back here."

The sliding door trundled shut. Amelia closed her eyes, sighing. Eventually Jordan would get over her anger. Then they could talk about it.

Chip began his nightly calisthenics, squirming, kicking. She tried talking to him, but he wouldn't settle. Finally, she opened her laptop again, began playing the videos Jordan had downloaded for her. The ones with Finn narrating. As always, the sound of his father's voice soothed Chip.

It had the opposite effect on Amelia.

When the beach scene with Jordan appeared, Amelia's vision blurred. And when his ink-stained palm showed up, her tears spilled over.

Finn took the front stairs that night after closing Fresh. He visited Jordan's room first, as usual. Standing in the doorway, staring at her empty bed, he just shook his head.

One of her socks lay half under the bed. He picked it up and tucked it in his back pocket.

He stood a lot longer in the opening to his bedroom. Without Amelia, it felt barren. Not at all the retreat it had been before her arrival. Not at all the welcoming place it had become with her in it.

Peeling down to his boxers, he tossed back the covers and slid between the sheets.

Her scent clung to them. He grabbed the second pillow, the one she'd used to prop herself up when she ate, and pressed his nose into it. Pomegranate body-wash.

Elke had brought different ones each week. But the pomegranate had been Amelia's favorite.

He wrapped his arms around the pillow. A poor substitute for her. His heartbeat thudded in his ears.

Suddenly Hayden's advice didn't seem all that on-target. Give her space? What the hell had he been thinking? But Greg had agreed. Apparently you could lead an independent woman to water, but you couldn't make her drink.

Downstairs in the kitchen, something creaked.

"Dammit." He'd forgotten to lock the back door. He reluctantly released the pillow, flung off the covers. The stillness in the house folded around him like a smothering cloak. He started down.

Between the landings, he paused.

The empty wall haunted him. No family pictures hung there, and it appeared none ever would.

He cocked back his arm and let fly, fist passing through the sheetrock like a wet paper towel.

Nursing his bleeding knuckles, he stared in satisfaction at the hole left behind.

That was more like it.

CHAPTER FOURTEEN

TWO WEEKS LATER, neither of them had blinked. Finn confronted his sister as Bethany blocked the doorway to Amelia's LDRP room.

"You're not supposed to be here! Don't make me call security on my own brother."

"You do what you have to do. I'll do what I have to do. And I have to see her." He gently grasped her arms and moved her aside.

"Amelia?" she called into the room, smoothing the sleeves of her coat when he released her. "You okay with this visitor?"

Amelia, wearing a hospital gown and bathrobe, sank into a gliding rocking chair with the assistance of a short, blonde woman in a tie-dyed T-shirt.

Amelia glanced at him warily, then back at Bethany. "Five minutes. He can have five minutes."

"Fair enough. I'll be back to make sure he leaves." Bethany wagged a finger at her. "And when I do, you're getting your butt in that bed so I can put the fetal monitor on you again. And don't give me any crap about being in bed for almost three months. I'm well aware."

"Fetal monitor?" He grabbed for Bethany as she went to leave. "Is everything okay with the baby? I mean, Amelia's only thirty-seven weeks..."

"Relax. It's routine. Chip's lungs will be fine because of the steroids Amelia's been getting." His sister glared at him. "Don't say or do anything to upset her. I'm going to pop down the hall and check on Elke."

Elke's husband, Jeremy, had texted Finn several hours after reporting Elke in labor, to alert him that Amelia had also shown up at the hospital in labor.

"Marie, would you get me more ice chips?" Amelia smiled weakly at the tie-dyed woman.

"Of course." Marie gave Finn a slow appraisal while she retrieved a little plastic bowl from a table by the bed.

"Who's that?" he asked when she'd left the room. "Doesn't dress like a nurse. Friend of yours?"

"She's my doula."

"Doula?"

"A professional labor companion."

"What?" He knelt in front of the rocking chair, placing his hands on her knees. "You hired a stranger to take care of you while you have our baby? Amelia, I told you, anything you need, I want to be there for you. That includes now."

"Yeah, just like you've been there for me the last two weeks, right?" The bitter edge to her voice knifed him in the gut. She didn't sound like a woman who'd learned to miss him in his absence.

"You *threw up* when I asked you to marry me. Man's entitled to be a bit put out by that."

"Maybe. But did it mean you had to put me out as well?"

"Does that mean you missed me?"

"The wound was just starting to heal, and here you are, ripping off the scab."

"I'm sorry." He stroked her leg. "I...had to see you. Make

sure you and Chip are okay." Finn laid both hands over her belly.

"You've seen me. Now get ou-oow. Damn!" She gasped, clenching her teeth so hard the muscle on the side of her face twitched. Her knuckles turned white as she gripped the arms of the chair. She closed her eyes.

Beneath his palms, her abdomen tightened like a steel band. His stomach twisted in sympathy. "What should I do? How can I help?"

She cracked open one eye. Her lips barely moved as she muttered, "Youcanshutup!"

"Just breathe." That's what people told women in labor, right?

Her other eye opened and she shot daggers at him. "I *am* breathing! Otherwise I'd be unconscious or dead." She groaned. "Both sound good right now."

The damn thing went on forever. Amelia's struggle through the pain touched him. This was the length she would go to for Jordan. Months stuck in a bed, the process of labor and delivery. Once more his admiration for her ratcheted up a notch.

Finally, the tension beneath his hands eased. Amelia's next exhale was longer, with a note of relief. Color flooded back into her knuckles and face; her whole body slumped deeper in the chair.

"Okay?"

"Ducky." She took another deep breath, followed by a slow release. "I only have hours more of this to look forward to. Spend months trying to keep him in, then work like hell to get him out."

Finn inched closer. "Chip, it's okay to come out now. Try to make this easy on your mother, will you?"

"Fat chance." She placed her hands on Finn's shoulders, shoved him backward. "You're in my space and breathing all my air."

"Sorry." He climbed to his feet. "Did Bethany say anything about his size? I mean...he's three weeks early. Is he going to be big enough for the transplant?"

"It's not like we have options. I can't cross my legs and keep him in there. Another match for Jordan isn't going to miraculously appear in the registry. I *have* to believe that after all this, yes, he's going to be big enough."

"Yes. Of course he is." Although Finn would like to back that conviction with some science. "How does this work? I mean, they'll collect the umbilical blood tonight?" He'd been well into dinner service when Jeremy had texted him. He'd left Marco cooking after admonishing the waitstaff to take no orders for risotto.

"As soon as he's born, yes. They'll collect the blood from the umbilical cord right here. It'll be processed and shipped to Portland, and then—"

"Whoa, wait a minute. Portland? I made all the arrangements for Dr. Wong to handle the transplant here."

Amelia cradled her belly in her hands. "And I unmade them. I'll be taking Jordan and the baby back to Maine as soon as your sister says we can leave. In about a week, she'll be back under the care of her original hematologist, and preparing for the transplant."

"But—"

"No buts." Amelia's expression was frosty. "Let me remind

you, these are *my* children. I will decide what's best for them. And what's best for Jordan is to return to her original care team for the transplant."

The muscles in Finn's neck knotted and his hands curled. "What happened to Jordan being *our* daughter?"

"You put me out! And now I'm doing the same to you. Get out! And don't come back!"

Bethany bustled into the room. "Sounds like your five minutes are up, Finn. You need to leave."

He backed toward the door, hands in the air. "Fine. I'll be in the waiting room."

Bethany advanced on him, pressing him until he finally stepped out into the hallway. "No, you won't. Because I can't trust you not to sneak in there and upset her again. I told you *not* to upset her. Can't you see the woman has enough going on without dealing with you?"

"But he's *my* son."

"And once he's born, you'll be allowed to see him. I told you, as long as he's inside her, he belongs only to her. I'll call you after the delivery."

"Any idea when that will be?"

She shook her head. "Babies have their own timetables. But it's going to be hours at least. I'd wager on tomorrow being his birthday."

"Can I at least see Elke before I go?"

"Elke's in no shape for visitors, either. You can see her after her boy is born, too." Bethany laid a hand on his arm. "I know it's hard."

Finn glanced down at the floor, cleared his throat against the sudden lump in it. "I—I wanted to be there. To see Chip born. I at least wanted to be in on the start of his life if she's going to take him away from me."

"I'm sorry it's not working out for all of you." His sister rubbed his shoulder. "I'll call you. Go home, Beginagain."

"Begin again." He snorted. Yeah, he wished he could rewind the last three months and start over.

In Fresh's private dining room, which, thankfully, had been unoccupied tonight, Finn shoved his empty glass across the white linen tablecloth at Hayden. "Another round, bartender."

Greg sat at Hayden's right, across the small table from Finn. A full glass of vodka occupied the only empty place.

A tribute to Ian, the missing of the Four Musketeers—the four middle Hawkins boys. A maudlin touch Finn had felt appropriate tonight.

Hayden, self-appointed guardian of the bottle, splashed more into the rocks glass.

Finn lifted it. "All for one and one for all."

Greg and Hayden repeated the toast, clinking their still very full glasses against his.

"I really 'preciate you guys bein' here tonight."

"Shut up," Hayden said. "No one likes a sappy drunk."

"I'm not drunk." The tightness in his chest that at times seemed like a vise grip crushing him had dulled only a little. Likewise, the image of Amelia's pained face, which had kept appearing in his mind, had only fuzzed, not vanished.

He drained the vodka. The ice cubes rattled when he slapped the glass down in front of Hayden again. "My son's birthday, and I'm not there." And given Amelia's intention to return to Maine with his children, it would likely be only the first of many birthdays, many other special moments he missed out on.

Greg and Hayden exchanged a look. Greg shrugged, then nodded. Hayden poured. "You're going to regret this in the morning."

"No, I won't. Just gotta get through tonight. Tomorrow I can go see my son. Bethany—*Dr.* Hawkins—said so."

"She's not going to let you near him if you're hungover," Greg said.

"I don't get hangovers. From vodka, anyway. Which is why we're drinking it." He squinted at his brothers' glasses. The booze level didn't seem noticeably lower in theirs. "You guys aren't keeping up. Not even close."

"I have to deal with a hundred teenagers at school—" Hayden glanced at his watch "—in six hours. The administration frowns on staff showing up reeking of alcohol."

Finn hoisted his glass again. "Sorry."

"S'okay. All for one, right?"

"Right." Finn slugged back two more gulps. "So, Greg, when are you and Shannon gonna have a kid of your own? I mean Ryan's great, but..."

Greg grinned. "As soon as I can convince her." He toyed with his glass. "She's preoccupied with the court stuff so we can adopt Ryan. But his father's an unexpected issue. You'd think being convicted of murdering your wife in front of your kid would automatically terminate your parental rights, but it doesn't. She and Cathy are petitioning the court to make that happen."

"You mean a murderer has more rights to his child than I do to Jordan? Crazy."

The door opened and Kara stepped in, a blue plastic Quickie Mart bag in her hand. "I got what you wanted, Finn. You can't honestly tell me you're going to eat this." She dropped the bag on the table in front of him.

"Yep. And if you tell anyone, you're fired."

"Ooh, I'm shaking. I've got another job, remember?" She leaned over, wrapped her arms around his neck and kissed his cheek. "Hang in there, big brother. Love you."

He patted her arms. "Back atcha."

"Night, guys."

Judging by Hayden's shifting expression as Kara left, Finn figured his little sister was making hand signals behind his back on her way out the door. He turned, but she was already gone.

The plastic rustled as Finn dug into the bag. He pulled out three packages, tossed one to each of his brothers. They tore them open. Finn sank his teeth into the spongy, cream-filled yellow cake. Despite the stiff texture, the preservatives, the fact that he could easily make far better, there was something comforting about scarfing down Twinkies with his brothers.

Especially Twinkies washed down with soul-numbing vodka.

Which blissfully had started to quiet the torment. Finn pillowed his head on his arm and closed his eyes.

"Think he's had enough now?" Greg asked.

"Looks like it. Let's pour him into bed so we can both get some sleep." The faraway sound of a chair pushing back from the table followed Hayden's response.

One on either side of him, his brothers hauled him to his feet. Which Finn did his best to move.

"Up, Finn. Lift your foot *up,*" Greg ordered when they got to the stairs.

"Oh, hell, I don't have the patience for this," Hayden said. He hefted Finn like a hundred pound sack of flour and draped him around his shoulders in a fireman's carry.

"Never leave a man..." Finn murmured.

"Semper fi, bro. Stay behind me, Greg."

"Like I'm going to catch you both if you go down with him? I don't think so."

The bobbing motion as they climbed the stairs made Finn's stomach queasy. He closed his eyes.

His next sensation was free-falling onto a mattress. Somebody tugged off his sneakers, which thudded on the floor.

Somewhere, a muffled cell phone rang. Finn's butt vibrated.

"Where the hell's his phone?" Greg asked. Hands patted down his front pockets.

"Roll him over. It's in the back."

Finn found himself flipped on his face. He moaned in protest.

"It's Bethany," Hayden said. "Is the baby here yet?"

Finn struggled to roll back over. Like a turtle stuck on its shell, it took him several tries.

"Elke's boy is? That's great." Silence passed. "You're kidding. Amelia changed her mind? Gotta tell you, that's not happening. He's in no shape to go anywhere right now. He's...kind of under the table."

"'Melia changed her mind?" A surge of hope flooded Finn.

He tried to sit up, but fell backward as the room started spinning. Blackness closed in from all sides.

Shitdamnhell...the oblivion he'd been seeking claimed him.

"He's not coming?" The shriekiness in her voice made Amelia cringe. She trembled, the sheets beneath her in the upright hospital bed soaked with sweat. "Why not?"

Bethany laid a calming hand on her shoulder. "Apparently he's had a little too much to drink tonight."

"That figures. That figures."

"Well, sometimes men do stupid things. As a chef, Finn loves his ale and wine, but he generally can hold his booze. It's not often he's drunk."

"Sure. Sure he's not. Doesn't matter. I asked him to come, and he's not coming. Figures." Fire flashed across her stomach as another contraction gripped her. Marie helped her roll to her side, and used a tennis ball to provide counterpressure to her lower back. By the time the contraction ebbed, panic had given way to defeat. "I can't do this. I can't do this. I'm done."

"Amelia, you can. You're almost there," Bethany soothed, stroking her hair. "Soon you can start pushing, and Chip will be here."

Amelia burst into tears.

Marie passed a picture of Jordan to Bethany. Bethany held it in front of Amelia's face. "For her, right, Amelia? This is all for her. You can do this."

Maybe Finn's inability to come was fate's way of keeping

her from making a bigger mistake.

Her uncertainty was washed away by the tidal wave of another contraction.

Finn leaned his head against the nursery window, hand splayed across the Plexiglas. On the other side, his son slumbered. In the next clear-plastic bed over, his son's cousin, Jeremy Kristoff, Jr., to be called JJ, squirmed despite being tightly wrapped in a blanket.

Finn didn't even know his son's name. They'd discussed it, but never come to an agreement on one. And now he had no idea what Amelia had chosen to call him.

Then again, it was going to be hard to think of him as anything other than Chip.

Finn had awakened late that morning, hangover free, but hazy on some of the details of the night. A voice mail from Bethany provided the details of his son's birth. She'd told him to come to the hospital during afternoon visiting hours, when all the babies would be in the nursery instead of their mothers' rooms. Finn had called his staff and given them the day off, then slapped a "Closed" and "It's a Boy" sign on the front door.

After that he'd contacted a florist and sent Amelia a dozen red roses. His next call went to his sister Cathy, a lawyer who specialized in family law.

"He's a fine-looking boy." Michael Hawkins clapped his hand on Finn's shoulder.

"He looks so small next to Elke's son." Compared to most of the babies in the nursery, actually.

"He's six pounds, two ounces. That's a fine size for thirty-seven weeks. Remember, JJ is only a few days from full term," Lydia said.

"Still..." The knot in Finn's stomach had nothing to do with what he'd consumed the night before, and everything to do with his worries about his son. And his daughter.

"He's big enough," Lydia murmured. "You have to have faith. We are *not* going to lose another one."

Michael crossed behind Finn to wrap his arms around his wife as she looked through the window. He nuzzled her ear.

Finn's chest tightened. He'd never expected to have what his parents had, not after two divorces. But now...he wanted it. More than anything else in the world.

And he wanted it with Amelia.

If that wasn't to be...

He stared at the two boys. Cousins born the same day. Three hours and change apart.

He vowed that whatever he had to do, his son would know his family. Know *him*.

Bethany rushed down the corridor, cheeks flushed, the edges of her coat flapping, exhaustion in her eyes. "Sorry I'm a little late. Got backed up at the office." She excused herself as she wound her way around several other family members gathered to gaze at the two babies, and pressed next to Finn. "So what do you think?"

"Is he okay? He looks so little."

"If he wasn't okay, he'd be in the NICU, not here. His Apgars were 9 and 10 out of 10. He's a miracle on so many levels. Come on." Bethany crooked her finger at him.

"Where are we going?"

"You want to hold him, don't you?"

"Absolutely."

Bethany led him to an empty LDRP room. Like the ones he'd seen Amelia in, it had glossy wooden floors, a green love seat under the window and a gliding rocking chair. The empty bed was covered with a green-and-yellow floral bedspread.

His parents settled on the love seat. Finn paced the small space while Bethany went to get the baby. She wheeled him into the room in his bassinet. "Sit down."

Finn sat in the rocking chair while his sister lifted Chip. "Make sure you support his head," she said, placing him in his arms.

"I've held a baby before, Bethany."

Warmth from the tiny wrapped bundle radiated against his chest. Brown peach fuzz passed for Chip's hair. Finn chuckled, caressing the down with one fingertip. It circled the baby's head, with sparse clumps on the top, like a balding man. "I hope this doesn't indicate what he has to look forward to later in life."

Chip yawned, then opened his eyes, looking up at Finn.

The hospital intercom chiming with pages, the murmur from the people in the hall by the nursery, even the presences of Finn's own parents and sister in the room faded. His focus narrowed until it was just him and his little boy. A mutual admiration society of two as they stared at each other. "Hey there, buddy. It's me. Daddy. Happy birthday, Chip. Sorry I'm a little late."

A flash shattered the moment, making them both blink, as Lydia captured the scene. Chip's nose scrunched up and his lower lip quivered.

Finn sucked in a deep breath. His son had Amelia's nose, and her eyes. If he only had some teeth to bite down on his lower lip...

"He looks like you," his mother said, leaning over to stroke Chip's cheek. The baby's head turned toward her finger, mouth working.

"Really? I was just thinking how much he looked like Amelia. And that seems only fair, given that she did all the work."

"You helped," Bethany said. "You took excellent care of his mother when she needed you."

Finn shrugged. "I suppose."

Lydia held out her hands. "Can I hold him?"

He tightened his grip for a moment. Then sighed. "Sure."

Bethany took the camera, snapping various poses. Chip with his grandparents. With his grandparents and father. It was the shot of three generations of Hawkins men that made Finn blink hard.

He cleared his throat. "I've got to talk to her, Bethany. And I'm taking our son with me."

His father transferred the baby to him. Then he cupped Finn's cheek, giving it a gentle tap. "Good for you. You fight. For all of them. I promise you, son, it's worth it. Don't you give up."

"No, sir." With Chip cradled firmly in his left arm, Finn strode down the hall to Amelia's room. He paused outside the door, dragged in a deep breath. Then he looked at the ceiling. "If you're listening...I could use some help here."

He rapped on the half-opened door, then went in.

Jordan lay curled on the love seat, her video camera on

the cushion, under her hand. She was asleep with her mouth slightly open. Amelia, partially upright in the bed, was also dozing. "Shhh," he said to Chip. "They're both sleeping."

He carried the baby across the room, then knelt in front of the love seat to look at Jordan. Her pasty skin made the dark smudges under her eyes stand out even more. Finn's stomach rolled. He hadn't seen her in over a week, since the last time he'd taken her to Dr. Wong's. She hadn't needed a transfusion that day, only platelets, but now...she really didn't look good.

"This is your sister, Chip. Have you met her yet? She's the princess you've come to save. Daddy's little hero."

He carried his son to the empty bassinet in the corner of the room, laid him inside. Then he eased down on the edge of the bed. Even in sleep, Amelia looked exhausted. He brushed the hair back from her forehead. Unable to stop himself, he leaned over and kissed her.

Her mouth softened beneath his lips. For a moment, she kissed him back. Then she inhaled deeply and her eyes flew open.

He drew away.

"You're kinda late, pal."

"You kicked me out."

"I changed my mind. A woman's allowed to change her mind when she's in labor."

"I'm sorry. I sent flowers." He offered her a hopeful grin.

"And they're very lovely. You were drunk?"

He shifted farther from her on the bed. "I was looking for a way to forget not being here with you. It seemed like a good idea at the time. It was killing me."

She shrugged. "Your loss."

"Yeah. It sure as hell was. Look, Amelia, I'm here to ask you, one more time. Don't leave me. Stay! Let Jordan have the transplant here, so I, so the whole family, can help. I mean, how are you going to take care of her, and take care of Chip at the same time?"

She blew out a long breath. "Finn...it's a done deal. The cord blood's been processed and shipped to Portland. As for Chip, I've already made arrangements with a nanny agency in Portland. Look, I have a life in Maine. I have a practice. *If* anything's left of it at this point. But it's how I support myself and my kids. What would you have me do? Just give all that up?"

"I can support you all. The restaurant's doing well—"

"How would you feel about giving up everything? Why don't I hear you saying you'll give up career and family to come to Maine with us? Why is it all about us sacrificing to stay here?"

Finn opened his mouth, but wasn't sure what to say. So he closed it.

"Exactly. That's what I thought." She took his hand. "Look, Finn, you're a really great guy. More prince than toad."

He groaned. "There's a big but coming after that."

The corners of her mouth lifted in a sad smile. "But I'm not marrying you. I'm not marrying anybody." She leaned around him to look at Jordan, then continued, more quietly. "About my reaction to your proposal...I was married once."

"What?" His eyebrows shot up. "All those times we talked about my marriages, and you didn't offer this information? Wait, don't tell me, you're still married." That idea left a bitter taste in his mouth.

"No. My so-called marriage turned out to be a sham in the

228

first place. I had it annulled because it made me feel better about it, but the truth is, it wasn't real. He'd used a fake identity." She shook her head. "It's still hard for me to talk about."

Finn squeezed her hand.

"He was a con man. He conned me into believing..."

"That he was a prince. That he loved you. That he'd take care of you." Finn lightly stroked her cheek. The final pieces to the puzzle of Amelia Young were sliding into place for him.

"Yeah."

"Then what happened?"

"He left me standing at a boarding gate at JFK, ready to take off for our honeymoon while he cleaned out my bank accounts and vanished."

His eyes widened, and his jaw went slack. He stared at her for a few moments. "Seriously?"

She nodded.

"Sounds like a bad made-for-TV movie."

"Welcome to my life. One bad made-for-TV movie after another."

"Damn. I swear, I'm going to find this guy and fillet him. I'm so sorry, babe." No wonder she prized her independence so much. His divorces made him feel like a failure, but he couldn't begin to imagine how a sham marriage would make him feel. Gun-shy for sure. "But I'm not him."

"I know that. At least, I think I do." She shrugged.

"So what happens now?" He wanted to tell her how much he loved her, but after her revelation, realized those words would fall on deaf ears. *Screw it.* "Amelia, I love you—"

"You don't even really know me."

"I know enough. You admitted I haven't seen you at your

best. If I can love you at your worst, don't you think I'd love you even more in normal times?"

She turned her head toward the doorway.

"Amelia...I'm not going away. I'm not a sperm donor anymore. I'm a real dad now. I love both these kids. Did you fill out Chip's birth certificate yet? You named me as father, right?"

Amelia sighed. She was so damned tired. Chip's birth had taken more out of her than she'd expected. "I haven't filled it out yet, no."

"But you'll put me down as his father, right? My sister Cathy says that if you don't, we can go before a judge to have it amended. Some paperwork, a paternity test and bingo. The state apparently loves to find fathers for children. And I will gladly pay whatever child support the court orders. He's my son, Amelia. I am not going to vanish from his life. I will be there for visitation, for holidays—"

"Slow down there, sport. Even if you get named as his father, how do you propose visitation with him? Every other weekend, like most daddies? That's a hell of a drive for you."

"I don't care. He's going to know me. And the rest of his family."

"And you're going to breast-feed him, too? Because he's going to be breast-fed for at least the first year of his life. Dads are important, but they can't do that."

His eyes narrowed. "Are you going to fight me on this? On being part of his life? Because I'm prepared to fight you. Cathy said we can even file for an injunction to prevent you from leaving the state with him."

Amelia recoiled. "You would do that?"

"I don't want to. We can be reasonable about this, right?"

"What about me, Dad?" Jordan appeared on the side of the bed, looking at Finn beseechingly. "You're gonna fight for me, too, right?"

"Aww..." He embraced her. Then he shifted so he could look at her. He stroked her hair. "I would if I could, sweetheart."

"But..." Jordan's bottom lip trembled. "Don't you want me, too?"

"Of course I do. But I signed paperwork before you were born. Legally, I don't have any claim to you."

"You're my dad." Jordan's face blanched even paler. "You're my dad! And you could fight for me if you wanted to!" She wrenched herself from his grasp and stumbled across the room, slamming the bathroom door. The lock snicked shut.

Chip started to wail.

Head pounding, Amelia pushed Finn off the edge of the bed as she jumped out of it. She lifted the baby—Charles Ian Paul Young, because thanks to Finn she couldn't stop thinking of him as Chip—from the bassinet, rocking him.

She spun on Finn. "Way to go. Make her think you don't want her. That's just what she needs to take with her into this transplant. She has a fight for her *life* ahead of her, and you're threatening me about Chip?"

"I *do* want her. And she's right. I should fight for her. Give me back my rights to her, Amelia. Amend *her* birth certificate. Name me *her* father, too."

"Are you crazy?"

"If a father wanting to be with both his children is crazy, then yeah, I'm crazy. Absolutely certifiable. I care enough about them both—"

"Save it. If you care enough, you'll at least give me time to get Jordan through her transplant and back on her feet before we divide up our son. I'm never changing Jordan's birth certificate." She pointed at the door. "Go, Finn. I'm leaving tomorrow—"

"You're driving sixteen hours two days after having a baby? Are *you* crazy? Why don't you let me—"

"Sia is flying down this afternoon. She bought a one-way ticket. She's doing the driving."

Sia had insisted. She'd been beside herself the whole time Amelia had been in Erie because she hadn't been able to visit. But Amelia had needed her a lot more in Maine, to take care of everything there.

"We'll stop in Portland on the way through to do Jordan's pretransplant testing. After that, depending on what tests they need and the results, we'll probably be home in Caribou for about two weeks, then back down in Portland for the transplant."

"You'll keep me informed about Jordan, right? I can call her? E-mail her?"

"If she *wants* to talk to you after this—"

He looked stricken.

Good. Served him right. "—I certainly won't stop her. I intend to give her every tool I can to make sure she wins this battle. Even if that means you."

Her daughter wanted to believe in him. Amelia could understand that.

She'd wanted to believe in him, too.

CHAPTER FIFTEEN

Day T+17 (17 days post-transplant)

THE ACHE IN HER BREASTS told time better than her watch. Amelia wearily pushed herself up from the recliner in the corner of Jordan's room at the bone marrow transplant unit.

Jordan's laptop, open on the adjustable bed table, blared Hawkins movies. Amelia had nicknamed it HTV—all Hawkins, all the time. She'd had no idea her daughter had gathered so much footage during their time in Erie, from the travelogues Jordan and Finn had made, to interviews with almost every member of the family, to Shannon and Greg's wedding.

If it comforted her, then Amelia wasn't about to protest.

Even if she could now narrate most of them by heart. Even if she suspected it was Jordan's subtle way of torturing her.

The images tugged at her. Finn's smile, his dancing with Jordan at the wedding, the beach scene...

Amelia missed him. Some days she felt as if she'd lost a limb. And the phantom pain sucked.

She paused by the bed. Jordan slept, her face flushed with fever, which thankfully had been lower at last check. Antibiotics dripped into her IV to help combat the mouth sores she'd developed. She'd also been given pain medication. Amelia stroked her daughter's head, fingers sliding over the silky scarf Jordan wore, even in this private place, to cover her hair loss.

That had made her sob more than any of the stressful procedures.

Amelia pulled a notecard out of the desk in the room, placed it on the table next to the laptop. *Gone to feed Chip. Be back soon.*

She struggled to balance her time between the kids, to nurse Chip at least twice for his daytime feedings, since he was getting the short end of the stick. Some days she worried her baby would forget who she was. Without her showing up to nurse him, he might have.

She scrubbed her hands before entering the anteroom, a chamber that acted as a buffer between Jordan's pressurized space and the outer unit. An additional germ barrier to protect her now even more fragile child. Once the inner doors closed behind Amelia, she could open the outer ones. Her chapped hands stung.

Outside, she gathered her purse and coat, pausing at the nurses' station to tell them she'd be gone temporarily. Before leaving the BMTU, she removed her blue paper booties, then went through a final set of doors, marked Exit Only. In the elevator, she leaned into the corner, fighting to keep her eyes open.

Outside, a cold wind blew her hair into her face. The afternoon sun struggled to break through the cloud cover. Amelia crossed the street to Daniel's House, a four-story building that rented furnished apartments to the families of children at the Portland Presbyterian Children's Hospital. A large portrait of the little boy, Daniel, whom the facility honored, hung on the wall near the elevators.

She joined another couple heading up. The man and woman wore the weary, shell-shocked expression Amelia had become all too familiar with. When the elevator stopped, she followed them off, turning left while they went right.

She slid the key into the lock. But it wouldn't turn. She wiggled it, tried the other direction, took it out and inserted it again. Finally, she rapped on the door, calling for the nanny. "Charlotte? Open the door. My key won't work."

A few moments later the door opened, revealing a middle-aged man with a balding head. He rubbed his eyes, then stared at her. "Can I help you?"

"You're not Charlotte."

"Nope. Can't say that I am."

Amelia glanced at the number beside the door. "Oh, I'm sorry." She sighed. "I got off at the wrong floor."

The man smiled wearily at her. "Happens to us all at some point. The absentmindedness of sleep deprivation."

Another short elevator ride, one floor up, and this time, as Amelia slid her key home and turned it, Chip's muffled cries penetrated the door. "I'm sorry, baby, I'm coming." She draped her coat over the island that separated the efficiency kitchen from the living room, and dropped her purse.

Charlotte, a chubby older woman, paced the floor, bouncing the crying baby in her arms. "Here's Mommy." Charlotte was actually her second nanny. Amelia had fired the first after a week when she'd discovered the woman's tendency to watch television all day and let Chip cry.

Amelia took her son, who immediately turned his face toward her chest.

"I thought we were going to have to tap the milk supply in the freezer again," Charlotte said.

"I was waiting for Jordan to fall asleep after the pain meds before I left."

Chip, frustrated by being so close and yet not being fed, scrunched his face up and burst into serious wailing.

Amelia carried him into the bedroom, stretching out in the middle of the king-size bed on her side. Chip latched on to her breast immediately.

Crying gave way to contented gulps.

He watched her, his brilliant blue eyes making her feel guilty every time she gazed into them. Like his big sister, Chip had his father's eyes.

Amelia was starting to realize she'd made a serious mistake.

She talked to the baby, telling him about Jordan's day so far, from the three spoons of applesauce and the ice pop she'd managed to get down for lunch, to the video greeting she'd received from her friend and crush, giver-of-the-awesomely-scary-exciting-first-kiss, Tyler. Ty e-mailed new videos on a regular basis, and they did the same, though Jordan preferred being the one holding the camera when she could manage it.

When Chip finished on one side, Amelie gathered him into her arms and repositioned them both on the other, placing a pillow between him and the edge of the bed.

Chip's sucking slowed. His eyes closed. He'd stop nursing for a few moments, then start again.

Amelia closed her eyes, too. Just a little rest.

In the space of several moments, she was asleep, dreaming about Finn's face, his smile, his voice.

"I love her because she's smart and funny. She's independent and strong—"

The doorbell startled her awake. She got up empty...aching...trying to remember the wisp of the dream, knowing only without doubt Finn had been involved.

Careful not to disturb Chip, she tucked him into the portable crib at the foot of the bed. She knuckled her eyes, then headed out.

Charlotte was closing the door. She held a vase with a bouquet of mini sunflowers, orange roses and lilies mixed with fall foliage. "I'll say this for him. The man is persistent." She handed Amelia the card, then set the vase on the counter.

"A little something to brighten your week. Thinking of you. Love, Finn."

Amelia's throat tightened. He'd sent flowers with the same message every Monday since Jordan's admission to the BMTU—where flowers and balloons weren't allowed because they gathered dust and germs.

"Too bad the goodies haven't gotten here yet," Charlotte said. "I'm craving chocolate." Every Thursday, like clockwork, brownies and other homemade treats appeared at the apartment, delivered by FedEx. He'd sent a football and a teddy bear for Chip's one month birthday.

Persistent didn't begin to cover it.

Consistent. Stable. Thoughtful. Wonderful.

Reliable...

Once again the idea that she'd made a horrible mistake, not just for herself, but for her children, gnawed at Amelia. Time away from him, not to mention the lessening of her anxiety and stress from both the pregnancy and Jordan's situation, had opened her eyes.

Every time he hadn't been there for her—putting her out of his house, not showing up at Chip's birth—that had been *her* fault, not his. She'd been the one to hurt him first. He hadn't abandoned her. She'd driven him away.

Because she'd been convinced he could be another Ron. That even if he wasn't, she somehow weakened herself by depending on him. Set herself up to hurt down the road...

A few hours later, after coaxing Jordan to eat some chicken soup and about a quarter of a chocolate milk shake, Amelia found herself rapping on the door of the unit's social worker, a warm, caring woman who invited her in.

"You just caught me. I was getting ready to head out for the evening." Though she kept seminormal hours, Helen gave cards with her cell number to all parents upon first meeting.

Amelia slumped in the chair in front of her desk. "I need somebody to talk to. I'm so damn confused."

"I'm all ears."

"Is there some kind of patient's-parent confidentiality here? If I spill my guts, you're not going to spread it around, right?"

Helen smiled. "As long as no one's going to get hurt if I don't."

So Amelia told her the entire story of Finn. A story that had begun over a year ago, when she'd shown up on his doorstep with a specimen cup and a small—in her opinion—request. She left out the more personal details, like losing her head in his kitchen. She talked about how he'd taken over caring for her, caring for Jordan, the whole thing.

Helen nodded when appropriate, made quiet noises of encouragement when Amelia faltered in the telling.

"So, what's your question?" she asked when Amelia finally fell silent.

She'd come to realize over the past few weeks that she loved Finn. But love wasn't the issue. "Is there really such a thing as too independent?"

Helen snorted. "I've watched you run yourself ragged, trying to take care of Jordan and that baby of yours, and you actually have to ask me that?" She leaned forward and pulled a pencil from the blue ceramic mug on her desk. "One pencil. Independent. All by itself." She snapped it in half. "Easily broken."

She pulled out two more. "Two pencils together. Sharing the load." This time the veins on the back of her hand stood out, she gritted her teeth, but neither broke. "See?" the woman asked. "They're stronger together, not weaker."

Amelia stared at the pencils for a moment, then slowly nodded her head. "Got it."

"Good. Now I have a question for you. Does this guy have any brothers? And are they available?"

Amelia grinned, her tension easing for the first time in weeks. "As a matter of fact…"

###

Finn glared at Tracey as she set a bowl of risotto back on the serving island. "Don't shoot the messenger." She raised her hands.

"What's the message?"

"Customer says it doesn't taste right."

"What the hell do you mean, it doesn't taste right?" He

grabbed a tasting spoon from the holder and dipped it into the dish. "Tastes fine to me. You taste it."

He handed her a clean spoon. Her nose wrinkled after she sampled it. "What?"

"It's a little bland. Needs more salt or something."

He sighed. Bland had been a complaint lately, but everything tasted right to him.

It was the world that was wrong. Bland. Lacking.

He fired up a replacement, this time adding salt slightly beyond what he thought it needed. When it didn't come back, he adopted the strategy for the rest of the service.

The kitchen cam and his laptop were both running. In case Jordan wanted to chat. Or just peek in on him. But she hadn't, to his dismay.

During the lulls, he rewatched the latest video from her on his laptop. Footage Jordan had shot from her hospital bed. The camera wobbled, then zoomed in on Amelia, sprawled in a recliner. Jordan's narration was hard to understand because of the sores in her mouth. "Here's Mom," she said. "Sleeping again."

He didn't catch the next sentence. But the images of Amelia tore at him. She'd lost all of the pregnancy weight. Maybe more. No longer radiant, she appeared wan. Pale.

There were moments when she looked almost as bad as Jordan.

She needed help, damn it. And he'd waited long enough for her to admit it. So, to hell with what she wanted.

When the final customer had left for the evening, and he'd turned the cameras off, Finn gathered his staff in the middle of kitchen cleanup. "Guys, I have an announcement. This was our last service for a while. I'm closing the restaurant. Hopefully temporarily, but..." He shrugged.

They stared at him as if he'd grown a second head.

"I need to help take care of Jordan and Chip," he explained. That brought nods of understanding. His staff had taken a shine to Jordan while she'd lived with him.

Kara clapped her hands. "About damn time."

"I'm sorry. I know the holidays are coming up. I'll pony up a month's severance. And I'll write you all excellent letters of recommendation—actually, Kara will." He looked at his youngest sister. "Okay?"

"Okay."

"I'll put out some feelers around town, pass on any leads. I'm sure you'll be working again in no time. And if I reopen, hopefully I can steal you all back from your new employers." In the morning he'd call his suppliers, stop shipments and deliveries. Hayden would keep an eye on the building. Sometimes it paid to have a brother living with you.

Without Amelia and the kids, the restaurant meant nothing, anyway. The goal he'd worked for his whole career, his own restaurant, and it didn't even come close to satisfying.

T+19 (19 days post-transplant)

It had taken him an entire day to get Fresh put to bed. Finn eased the Explorer off the highway into a rest area on the Massachusetts Turnpike. They'd been on the road since 5:00 a.m., and according to the navigation on his phone, had only about two more hours in the ten-and-a-half-hour trip to Portland. He'd hoped to make it without too many delays, but his butt had gone numb. He needed more than a quick bathroom break or gas tank refueling. "Let's grab lunch, huh, Mom?"

She nodded. "Sounds like a plan. I'm hungry." His mother had insisted on accompanying him to Maine to help care for Jordan and Chip. Other members of the family had also offered to rotate to the hospital to lend support.

Amelia didn't know it, but reinforcement troops were about to land.

Finn settled a baseball cap—swiped from Hayden—on his head. Sliding from the driver's seat, he went around to the back of the SUV and raised the door. He dragged the cooler to the edge of the cargo space and opened it as his mother joined him. "What do you want? Roast beef and provolone on a sourdough roll, or grilled turkey and Monterey Jack with cranberry sauce on a kaiser?"

She smiled. "Have I mentioned that I like road-tripping with you? The food sure beats what they serve in there." She jerked her thumb in the direction of the plaza building. "I'll take the turkey, please."

"Of course it does." Finn eased aside the pumpkin pie he'd made for Amelia, now that pumpkins were readily available. He grabbed two wrapped sandwiches, two bottles of water, and closed the cooler. Then he picked up his laptop, which he slung over his shoulder. "It's too cold to eat out here. Let's go inside. I want to check my e-mail, anyway, see if there's anything new from Jordan."

"You didn't tell her we were coming, did you?" His mother fell into step with him as they crossed the parking lot. A crisp wind rustled dried leaves along the blacktop.

"No. I want to surprise her and Amelia."

"I hope you know what you're doing."

"What's that supposed to mean?" He held the door for her, releasing the warmer air from inside.

"I just hope you—we'll—be well-received. She wasn't thrilled with you when she left, and I'm afraid she might feel the same way about me."

Finn slid into a booth in the food court, setting his laptop on the seat beside him and unzipping his jacket. "What's that mean, Mom? What did you do?"

"Nothing. I just told her she was passing up an amazing guy. And it wasn't fair to her children to be raised so far from the family who loves them."

Finn groaned. "Mom."

"Sweetheart, you can understand now what it's like to be separated from your children. It doesn't hurt any less because it's a grandchild." His mother sighed, staring at her sandwich.

"Hey." He waited for her to meet his gaze. "Are you sure you're going to be okay seeing Jordan in the bone marrow transplant unit?"

She nodded. "Absolutely. I can do this."

He smiled. "Okay." He didn't want to bring back too many memories of Ian for her, and how he hadn't lived long enough to make it into the transplant unit.

"Eat your lunch, Finnegan, and let's get back on the road."

"Yes, ma'am." While he did, he hauled out his laptop, powering it up and connecting to the free Wi-Fi. Almost at once, e-mail messages began to come in, including one from Amelia with an attachment. The downloading icon indicated more on the way, but he opened Amelia's first.

Finn, these papers are necessary to take care of this. They must be signed in the presence of a notary, and we'll need a DNA test to prove her paternity.

He stopped reading there. A DNA test? He clicked on the attachment.

And had to force the bite of sandwich past a sudden lump in his throat.

"Finn? Is something wrong? Something about Jordan?"

He shook his head. Then he nodded. He cleared his throat. "Amelia...sent me paperwork, Mom. She's amending Jordan's birth certificate to name me as father."

His mother beamed at him. "That's wonderful news."

"Yeah." An incredible gesture on her part. He was officially going to be more than a sperm donor. He was truly going to be Jordan's dad.

So why did that still leave him feeling only partially satisfied?

Because he wanted it all. Greedy, yes. But he wasn't going to rest until he convinced Amelia that he should be in *her* life as well.

The final e-mail finished downloading. It was from Amelia with another attachment. A big attachment, judging from the download time.

Finn—I'm going to let this video speak for itself. I hope you believe in forgiveness. In second chances.

Second chances? Heart thudding, he plugged in his earphones, tucked them into his ears, then clicked open the video.

The camera panned around Jordan's hospital room. Amelia narrated. "This is Jordan's room here at Portland Presbyterian Children's Hospital." Amelia's hand moved in front of the lens. Everything went blurry for a moment, then the camera autofocused. On her palm, in black ink, was "Wish you were here."

Finn held his breath. The scene flashed to a sign marked 407. "This is my apartment." The door opened, and the field wobbled as she walked inside. "This isn't much like your kitchen, but..." She set the camera on a countertop and again stuck her hand in front of it. The letters were fainter, but the message was still loud and clear. *Wish you were here.*

Warmth radiated from the center of his chest. Amelia showed him the living room, Chip's crib, and then finally settled on a bed. She patted the floral bedspread, then flashed her palm one more time.

She didn't just need him. She *wanted* him.

She turned the camera around so her face filled the frame. "I was a fool. A stubborn fool who was so afraid of getting hurt. I hope you can forgive me. If you can...you know where to find me. Us."

The video went black.

She hadn't mentioned love. But he'd take what she was offering. Elated, he slammed his laptop closed. "Grab your stuff, Mom. Let's finish eating on the road."

"Why the rush? Something wrong?" She immediately began wrapping her sandwich.

He again shook his head, a huge grin lifting his mouth and his spirits. "No. Something very right."

Fortunately, he made good time on the highway. Because

once reaching the hospital, Finn discovered the process for getting into the BMTU was excruciatingly tedious.

Three hand-washings, a pair of paper booties, a health questionnaire and interrogation by a nurse later, Finn left his coat and cap on a shelf outside Jordan's room. The volunteer staffing the front desk downstairs had confirmed Amelia's presence. His mom had to wait in the lobby, since only two visitors were allowed in a BMTU patient's room at a time—and the rules were strictly enforced.

Finn stepped into the anteroom. Through the glass, he could see Jordan in her bed. He went to the sink, washing his hands again as instructed.

He craned his neck to see Amelia sprawled in the recliner, eyes closed. She was probably used to the medical staff coming and going. And she'd learned to sleep when Jordan did. He went to his daughter first, hunching down alongside the bed. "Hey there. You gonna wake up and say hello to me? Pretty sad thing, I come all this way and my two girls are both sleeping."

Jordan's eyes opened. Widened. "Dad." Her grin turned to a grimace, and she winced, covering her mouth briefly. "You're here!"

"I am."

"Ohmigod. What happened to your hair? Daddy, you're bald!"

"Shhh. Don't wake your mom. What, you don't like it? Uncle Hayden said it makes me look tough. Scary."

Jordan giggled, again covering her mouth. "I don't think he meant scary in a good way."

"Oh, thanks a lot. Here I shave my head to prove to you it's only hair, and that's what I get for my trouble." Finn stroked the silk covering she wore over her own head. Brown peach fuzz, visible around the edges of the scarf, had started to grow back. "No fair. I think you have more hair than I do."

"Chip has more than both of us."

"That's okay. I'm sure we'll both have a full head again long before he does."

Jordan held open her arms. Hesitantly—the wires and tubes connected to her made him nervous, especially the one in her chest—he gathered her into a hug.

"I'm not gonna break," she whispered.

Finn blinked hard. "No, course not. You're the tough one in the family. I guess this means you're not mad at me anymore?" He released her.

She shook her head. "No. I got over that the day we left. But...I've been fighting for you."

"You have? How's that?"

The corners of her mouth edged up in a tightly controlled smile. "For one thing, I've been playing your videos over and over. Especially the one where you say you love Mom."

"I don't remember that."

She looked sheepish. "I thought I had the camera turned off. But it caught the audio. The day you made us leave? I asked if you loved Mom?"

Finn chuckled, taking Jordan's hand. "Well, whatever you did, it worked. Your mom should have been more careful when she taught you to always have a plan, huh? Now I'm going to wake the other sleeping beauty."

He knelt beside the recliner, just staring, drinking his fill after being deprived of her for almost eight long weeks. Then he leaned forward and pressed his lips against hers.

She sighed in her sleep. Then her mouth began to move beneath his. Her hand came up to cup the back of his head.

And her eyes flew open.

He backed away, grinning.

"Finn! Oh, your hair," she whispered. "Your beautiful hair." Her lower lip quivered.

"It's only hair. It'll grow back. That was the point."

She bit her lip.

"You've gotta stop doing that. You'll make it bleed." He brushed his fingers over her mouth. "You'd seriously cry over hair?"

She shook her head. "No. Over a wonderful man who would shave his head for his daughter. And be-because I've been so stupid. I need you, Finn. *We* need you. And—and...I love you."

She loves me. The realization thrilled him.

She started babbling about pencils, and being stronger with two instead of one, and tears actually started to fall.

Jordan giggled behind him from her bed as her mother melted down.

"I think your mom is a bit overtired, Jordan."

"I'll say."

"I— I'm not making any sense, am I?" Amelia asked.

He shook his head. "Nope. But it's okay. You had me at 'I love you.'" He started to gather her into his arms, but she pushed against him.

"I don't know about marriage. I'm not sure I can do that. You okay with that?"

"Sweetheart, if you won't make an honest man of me, I

will shack up with you for the rest of my days if that's what you want. I'm sure my mom will have a few things to say about it, but..." He shrugged. "She'll get over it. If you give the word, I'll spend my days cooking at a greasy spoon diner in the north woods of Maine, as long as I can come home at night to you and our kids."

"I don't think we have to get that drastic. You're a chef, not a cook. Except for maybe at home. And we can decide where that will be later." She glanced at her watch. "Hey. How did you get here so fast? I only sent those e-mails a few hours ago."

Finn took her red, rough hand in his, turning it over. The words had been scrubbed clean by the numerous hand-washings she'd endured since the morning. But he pressed his lips to where they'd been. "You wished me here."

Heart full to the point she feared it would burst from her chest, Amelia caressed the smooth surface of his head. Though she missed being able to run her fingers through his thick, dark hair, she had to admit the gesture had been the final proof.

Finn Hawkins was no toad. And was worthy of her trust. Her love.

And their children.

EPILOGUE

T+339 (339 days post-transplant)

HAWKINS FAMILY CHAOS in Fresh's dining room. Amelia wasn't sure she'd ever get used to it, to the level of noise they could generate, to the amazing joy she felt in the midst of all these people. She'd made the right call months ago, asking Finn to be part of her life.

And then again when she'd opted to study for the PA Chiropractic Boards and relocate to Erie, so her children could have the rich experience of being part of the large, close-knit group. Chip's cousin JJ could be the brother he would never have.

Because despite Finn's occasional, half-serious attempts to cajole her into having another one, her baby days were over. One insane pregnancy like Chip's had been more than enough.

Though the benefits had far outweighed the drawbacks.

Seeing Shannon, now six months pregnant, press a hand to her back and sink down into a chair was enough to remind Amelia she didn't want to do it again, even if she could avoid a bed-sentence.

Greg shot to his wife's side in an instant, full of concern as he knelt beside her. Ryan, Shannon's nephew, also rushed to her. They'd finally gotten the go-ahead to adopt the boy. The paperwork would be finalized next month.

A cheer from the center of the room diverted Amelia's attention as her son—*their* son—toddled three wobbly steps from the security of his father's grasp toward his grandmother's open arms.

Their son's first steps.

Finn jumped to his feet, flashing a triumphant grin her way. He'd been coaching Chip for days.

"Thank you," he mouthed, then flashed *I love you* in sign language—something else he was teaching their son, after reading an article about it on the Internet.

She sighed. A year later, and Finn could still melt her heart with his joy at being with them.

The tables in Fresh's dining room had been shoved along the walls, making space in the middle of the room for the birthday festivities. One table held a mound of presents, another featured a bowl of red frothy punch Finn had created, along with an assortment of the delicious finger foods he'd spoiled her with during her bed rest. Two separate cakes—one the figure of a superhero, the other a dog—adorned another table.

JJ and Chip, the birthday boys, posed in front of the fireplace. Each straddled a plastic ride-on fire engine, with Michael and Lydia on either side, while so many flashes burst from different cameras the paparazzi might as well have crashed the party.

Derek's daughters, Katie and Lila, ran past Amelia, the younger one pausing to sneeze. Amelia froze.

Finn came up behind her, slipping his arm around her waist and pulling her against him. "She's not sick. They're all well aware of the rules. The kid has fall allergies. Give her a break." He nuzzled her ear. "Besides, Jordan just started school again. *Without* her mask. Her counts are good. She's going to run into germs at school. *High* school." He groaned. "We are the parents of a one-year-old and a high school freshman."

"Soon to be the parents of a toddler and a teen about to drive. The worst of both ages."

"Something to look forward to." Finn touched the tip of his tongue to the lobe of Amelia's ear, sending heat through her. A year later and he could still melt the rest of her, too.

"I'm looking forward to our own party later," he said.

"You are, huh?"

"I am. I have a surprise for you."

Amelia chuckled. He'd cured her surprise phobia for good. Now, she always looked forward to whatever he had up his sleeve. "I'll just bet you do, sport."

"Ohmigod. Will you two cut it out?" Jordan said, suddenly appearing beside them. "There are little kids around, in case you missed it. Birthday party? Babies?"

"Go get your picture taken with your brother," Finn ordered. "After all, you're the reason he's here."

She smirked at him. "We couldn't have done it without you, Dad."

"Smart aleck," he muttered, then raised his voice. "That's right. You owe me your life twice over, kiddo. Which means you'll listen when I lecture you on the evils of teenage boys."

She stuck her tongue out at him, then crossed to join the photofest, video camera raised up to capture the image of Chip giving JJ a slobbery kiss—the only kind Chip gave—on the cheek.

Amelia laughed, fingering the necklace Finn had given her as a gift on Chip's real birthday, four days earlier. The word *Mom*, in silver, repeated over and over in a circle representing, he'd said, the eternal nature of a mother's love. Each O held a little white crystal.

"Did you want to announce our news?" she asked.

"Not today. This is the boys' day. Let's save it for next Sunday's family dinner." He turned her around to face him. "You're sure about it, right? Because once we tell my mom that you intend to make an honest man out of me, and that you want the whole nine yards—the big church wedding with the whole family present—there's no going back. You'll be stuck on that course for good. My mother and sisters will flay you alive if you try to back out."

She leaned into him, kissed him. "I'm sure. I'm ready."

Hours later, when the extended family had cleared out, while Amelia was putting the kids to bed—as much as anyone actually "put" a teenager to bed—and the dining room had been restored for the next day, Finn climbed the back staircase.

He paused between the landings, where a series of photos hung on the wall. Chip's hospital picture. A photo of Jordan, wearing a mask, holding Chip in the apartment the day she'd been released from the BMTU and reunited with her little brother, her hero.

Finn and Amelia, the night she'd announced they would call Erie home. That one had been a huge, but very welcome, surprise.

All four of them on the front porch steps, shot by Hayden, the day they'd arrived.

A photo of Finn, wearing his Kiss the Cook apron, sleeping on the sofa in the master bedroom, Chip snuggled on his chest.

Soon enough they'd add a wedding picture to the family gallery.

They might have gotten the order wrong. But they'd gotten the family right.

Dear Reader,

I hope you enjoyed returning to the Hawkins family as much as I did. After writing *A Hero to Keep,* I knew Greg's siblings had to have stories of their own, and I'm pleased to share Finn's with you.

Stories that involve assisted reproduction fascinate me. Partly because I've experienced fertility issues, but I think what fascinates me the most is the emotional aspect. When people talk about assisted reproduction, you hear a lot about science and morality. But you don't hear a lot about the emotions that come into play.

And there are plenty of emotions involved—love, fear, hope, sorrow, joy....

I've wanted to tell a savior sibling story for years, ever since I heard the story about parents who, before preimplantation genetic screening could guarantee a match, rolled the dice and had another child to save their daughter from leukemia—and succeeded.

Hayden Hawkins is next in line, so keep an eye out for his story.

I'd love to hear from you! Please visit my Web site, www.susangable.com and join my newsletter so you get extra bonus materials and other fun things like contests. E-mail me at Susan@susangable.com. Or like my Facebook page! (Facebook.com/SusanGableAuthor) Although Amelia has ambivalent feelings about Facebook, I happen to adore it and have a lot of fun there. Please join me!

Susan Gable

About the Author

Visit www.SusanGable.com and **sign up** for her **newsletter** so you don't miss out on great stuff, including **special freebies** only for subscribers!

Email Susan@SusanGable.com. She'd love to hear from you!

If you've enjoyed this book, **please consider leaving a review** on the e-tailer where you purchased it! Reviews matter a lot for writers. Please and thank you!

Susan Gable was born with a book in her hand.

Okay, that may be a slight exaggeration, but not by much. Her love of books goes back to her preschool days, when books arrived at her house from the Weekly Reader Book Club. Some of them even had records so she could listen to the stories! (Remember records?)

Both of Susan's parents are voracious readers, and they infected her as well.

Susan shared her love of reading (and Weekly Reader!) as an elementary teacher for ten years, then turned to writing after a year of homeschooling her son caused her to nearly lose what was left of her mind. Writing, it turns out, is cheaper than therapy, and homeschooling is far harder than teaching other people's kids.

That son is now grown (Susan's not sure how that happened, as she feels no older than the day she first started writing).

Susan's books have been Golden Heart and Rita ® Award finalists, been recognized by Romantic Times nominations for Best Superromance of the Year, and she's won numerous awards, including the National Readers' Choice Award. She's been praised by readers and reviewers alike for her ability to tell emotionally compelling stories that make them laugh and cry.

Close to a half million copies of her books have been sold worldwide.

More Hawkins Books

Coming soon! Hayden's story, *A Promise to Keep*.

Have you read Greg and Shannon's story, *A Hero to Keep*?

Sometimes you have to fight for what - for who - you love.

Shannon Vanderhoff's childhood taught her early on that nothing was hers to keep, not clothes, or toys, or even people. So she lives, loves, and lets go. She's not looking for a hero.

But with custody of her traumatized six-year-old nephew on the line, she needs help. Charming Greg Hawkins, a comic book artist and art therapist insists he can coax Ryan into speaking again, enabling the boy to reveal what he saw the night of his mother's death at his father's hands. And though Shannon's skeptical of Greg's methods, there's no denying that he brings light and color to their lives.

Greg, one of twelve siblings, knows anything worth having is worth fighting for. If anyone can prepare Shannon for the upcoming battle, it's Greg and his family.

But will she fight to keep him, too?

A Hero to Keep is a contemporary family drama romance set near Lake Erie, featuring the Hawkins Family. Grab your copy today!

"Emotionally charged scenes and a terrific plot make this novel a must-read. Gable's writing is clever, and the emotions she portrays are exceptionally realistic." - 4.5 Stars, Top Pick Alexandra Kay - Romantic Times BOOKreviews Magazine

28734450R00143

Made in the USA
Columbia, SC
16 October 2018